# Table of Contents

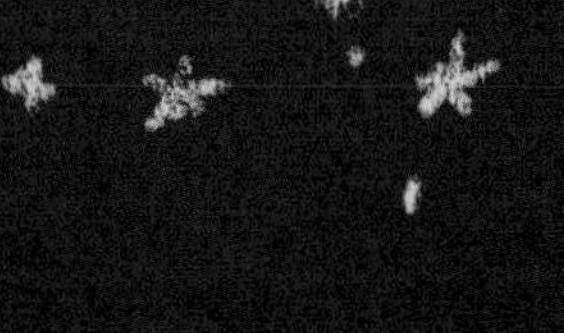

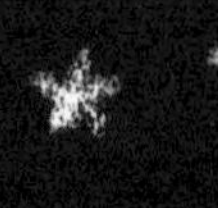

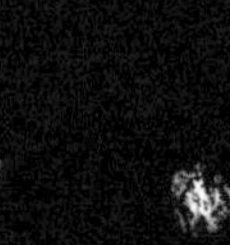

# One Minute till Bedtime

60-SECOND POEMS TO SEND YOU OFF TO SLEEP

Selected by KENN NESBITT

Art by CHRISTOPH NIEMANN

Little, Brown and Company
New York Boston

For Kinsey
—KN

For my grandmother Maria and her countless bedtime stories
—CN

This book was edited by Susan Rich and designed by Phil Caminiti and Nicole Brown with art direction by David Caplan. The production was supervised by Erika Schwartz and Ruiko Tokunaga, and the production editor was Andy Ball. This book was printed on 140 gsm Gold Sun Woodfree paper. The type is Museo Slab. The illustrations were rendered using handmade and digital media.

 • Little, Brown and Company • Hachette Book Group • 1290 Avenue of the Americas, New York, NY 10104 • Visit us at lb-kids.com • Little, Brown and Company is a division of Hachette Book Group, Inc. • The Little, Brown name and logo are trademarks of Hachette Book Group, Inc. • The publisher is not responsible for websites (or their content) that are not owned by the publisher. • First Edition: November 2016 • Copyright acknowledgments can be found on pages 166–68. • Library of Congress Cataloging-in-Publication Data • Names: Nesbitt, Kenn, editor of compilation. | Niemann, Christoph, illustrator. • Title: One minute till bedtime : 60-second poems to send you off to sleep / (edited) by Kenn Nesbitt; illustrated by Christoph Niemann. • Description: New York : Little, Brown and Company, [2016] • Identifiers: LCCN 2015040416 | ISBN 978-0-316-34121-9 (hardcover) • Subjects: LCSH: Children's poetry. • Classification: LCC PN6110.C4 O525 2016 | DDC 821.008—dc23 • LC record available at http://lccn.loc.gov/2015040416 • 10 9 8 7 6 5 4 3 2 1 • APS • PRINTED IN CHINA

# Whew!

Finished dinner.
Cleared my plate.
Took the trash out.
Shut the gate.
Had a bath and
brushed my teeth;

those on top
and underneath.
Telephoned
my gramps and grammas.
Changed into
my soft pajamas.
Fluffed the pillows.

Got my Ted.
Said my prayers.
Climbed in bed.
All that's done;
at last I'm freed.
*Finally,*
it's time to read.

—*Kenn Nesbitt*

# Paper People

Every book you've ever read
makes a home inside your head.

Characters that you adore
gather round your noggin's floor.

You travel widely with each one
and do the things that each has done.

Their paper lives are fragile, true...
The reason they exist is YOU!

*—Lisa Wheeler*

# I Like Old Stories

I like old stories. I'm amazed
by fairy tales from olden days,
when girls and boys got lost in woods
and ran around in riding hoods.

In dusty storybooks, I love
to gaze at inky drawings of
enchanted castles, clanking chains,
pirate treasure, wagon trains,
deep-sea-diving submarines,
dinosaurs and time machines.

Maybe every tattered page
was loved by someone just my age,
perhaps a boy—who now is grown—
and writes new stories of his own.
I'm fine with that, because it's true:
Grand old stories once were new!

*—Kim Norman*

# If I Were a Blue Balloon

If I were a blue balloon,
I'd lift you up to fly with me
through silver starlight, past the moon—
I'd share my nighttime willingly.

I'd lift you up to fly with me
where dragons set the sky aflame.
I'd share my nighttime willingly.
You'd be a knight and lay your claim
where dragons set the sky aflame.
I'd ferry you through dreams of night—
you'd be a knight and lay your claim!—
then float you into morning light.

I'd ferry you through dreams of night,
through silver starlight, past the moon,
then float you into morning light—
if I were a blue balloon.

*—Renée LaTulippe*

# Roar

Lions roar
Big jaws, yellow eyes
Sharp claws, iron thighs
Everyone races away

Except those who stay to play
On his back and neck
And with his long strong tail

Daddy is Daddy, after all.

*—Donna Jo Napoli*

# Stuffed Animal Collection

A lion. A hippo.
A penguin. A fox.
A camel with bells on.
A zebra that rocks.
A giraffe and a monkey.
A gray kangaroo.
Mom calls it my bedroom.
I call it my zoo.

*—Eileen Spinelli*

# Five Little Birds

Five little birds in New York City,
Five little birds sit nice and pretty,
Five little birds sing a doo-wop ditty,
Five little birds in New York City.

*—Charles Waters*

# Pigeon

The pigeon is so cheerful
next to other birds you meet.
He bobs his head and steps
like he's dancing to a beat.
Other birds build nests in trees;
the pigeon likes concrete.
Other birds pick berries;
the pigeon picks the street.
Popcorn, pretzels, bits of bread—
he loves leftover treats.
No wonder he looks happy
to everyone he greets.

*—Jacqueline Jules*

# Me at the Sea

The sea comes *in,*
the sea goes *out.*

It tickles at my toes.
It buries my feet
in soft wet sand

as *in* and
*out* it goes.

The sea comes *in,*
the sea goes *out.*

It scatters birds on shore.
It brings me gifts of
scalloped shells

as *in* and
*out* it flows.

*—Betsy Franco*

# Ocean Fun

**A** sun-stung
**B**oy
**C**ools down for the
**D**ay—
**E**ach freezing step
**F**lings a
**G**lacial spray.

**H**ow
**I**cy the
**J**olt as this
**K**id
**L**eaps about,
**M**aking
**N**ew waves
**O**n his
**P**lunge in and out!

**Q**uickly he races
**R**ight into the
**S**ea:
**T**oes, ankles, shins, then
**U**p to his knee—
**V**aults into
**W**ater
**X**-ploring new turf,
**Y**et thrilled to be chilled and
**Z**apped by the surf.

*—Avis Harley*

# Water Can Be a…

drip dropper
floor mopper
toilet flusher
hydrant gusher
earth drencher
thirst quencher
Ahhhhhhhhhhh!

*—Carol-Ann Hoyte*

# Gentle Shower

Little raindrops:
Through the glass,
See the raindrops—
Watch them pass.
*Let's go out!*

Little raindrops,
Feel them land
On your head,
On your hand.
*Let's go in!*

*—Edel Wignell*

# Backyard Circus

Apples, apples,
juggle, toss.
If you drop one,
applesauce!

*—Nikki Grimes*

# Trampoline

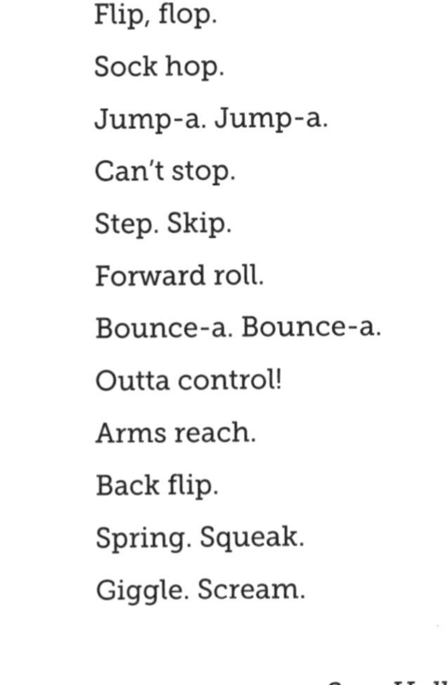

Flip, flop.
Sock hop.
Jump-a. Jump-a.
Can't stop.
Step. Skip.
Forward roll.
Bounce-a. Bounce-a.
Outta control!
Arms reach.
Back flip.
Spring. Squeak.
Giggle. Scream.

*—Sara Holbrook*

# Map of Fun

Where did my feet walk today?
Did they step on a cloud, or into a sea?
Did a smooth wooden floor
welcome their beat?
They slid through the grass,
they stepped on a stone.
I dashed up the stairs.
My cat bit my toe.
I slid in the hall.
I splashed in a bath.
My fabulous feet felt it all.
Now they are curling under the sheet.
Tomorrow I will dance and run.
Skip and hop. Twirl and leap.
Feet always find the map of fun
and follow it.
But now, they rest,
they rest.

*—Naomi Shihab Nye*

# Sleepy

I'm ever so sleepy.
I can't stay awake!
The drowsiness might be
Too heavy to take.

My eyelids are falling.
I'm feeling too weak
To open them anywhere
Close to their peak.

I cannot avoid it.
I'm falling asleep.
I've started unconsciously
Counting my sheep.

My brain has begun
To shut down in my head.
But please, Mother, don't make
Me crawl into bed!

*—Santino Panzica*

# Wave Good Night

Rub your eyes, you sleepyhead,
the dark is all you'll miss.
Tuck your fingers into bed,
just inside your fists.

Pointers, middles, rings—good night.
Sleep tight, pinkie ones.
Sweet dreams, fingers, left and right.
See you later, thumbs.

*—Michael J. Rosen*

# The Road to Morning

Of all the roads that roam the night,
curving left and swerving right,
none can twist itself so tight
as the zigzag road to morning.

For many a moon this road has swirled
and whirled and wound around the world.
And many a kid has spun and twirled,
lost on the road to morning.

It's a dizzy road, for sure. But then
it always gets you home again.

*—Kurt Cyrus*

# My Horse Is Floating in the Air

My horse is floating in the air
Above the tallest trees,
While I relax upon his back
And feel the morning breeze.

I don't know what his secret is,
But I am glad, of course,
To be the one who gets to ride
The only floating horse.

*—Jack Prelutsky*

# The Big Parade

A centipede sat
　By the side of the road.
Along came a turtle,
　Along came a toad.

The turtle was singing
　A rock 'n' roll song,
The toad did a flip
　As she boogied along—

And the centipede danced
　In a centipede way;
He wiggled his hips,
　And he cried, "Hip-hooray!"

*—Dennis Lee*

# All at Once

All at once upon a time
Goldilocks called on the Three Little Pigs,
The Troll found the Three Bears' porridge too hot, too cold, and just awful,
And the Wolf huffed and puffed the Three Billy Goats right off the bridge.

Hansel climbed the Beanstalk,
Jack ate the Pea,
The Princess met all Seven Dwarves.

The Frog kissed the Shoemaker,
The Elves scrambled the Golden Egg,
And Beauty took off with Rumpelstiltskin.

Midnight, struck the clock.

The Fairy Godmother waved her magic wand,
Transforming the Ugly Duckling
Into Stone Soup.

And everyone lived
Oddly
Ever
After.

*—Jon Scieszka*

# Poems Can Be Silly

Poems can be silly, Ted.
Poems can be serious.
Some are clear and simple,
while others are mysterious.
Some of them are rhyming,
though some of them are not.
Some will tell a story,
and some will share a thought.
Some will paint a picture
to keep inside your mind.
But all of them are treasures, so
let's see what we can find.

*—Kenn Nesbitt*

# Dinnertime

My father tells me that it's rude
To play with all my dinner food
Too bad for Dad, I cannot hear
I have a carrot in each ear

*—Scott Seegert*

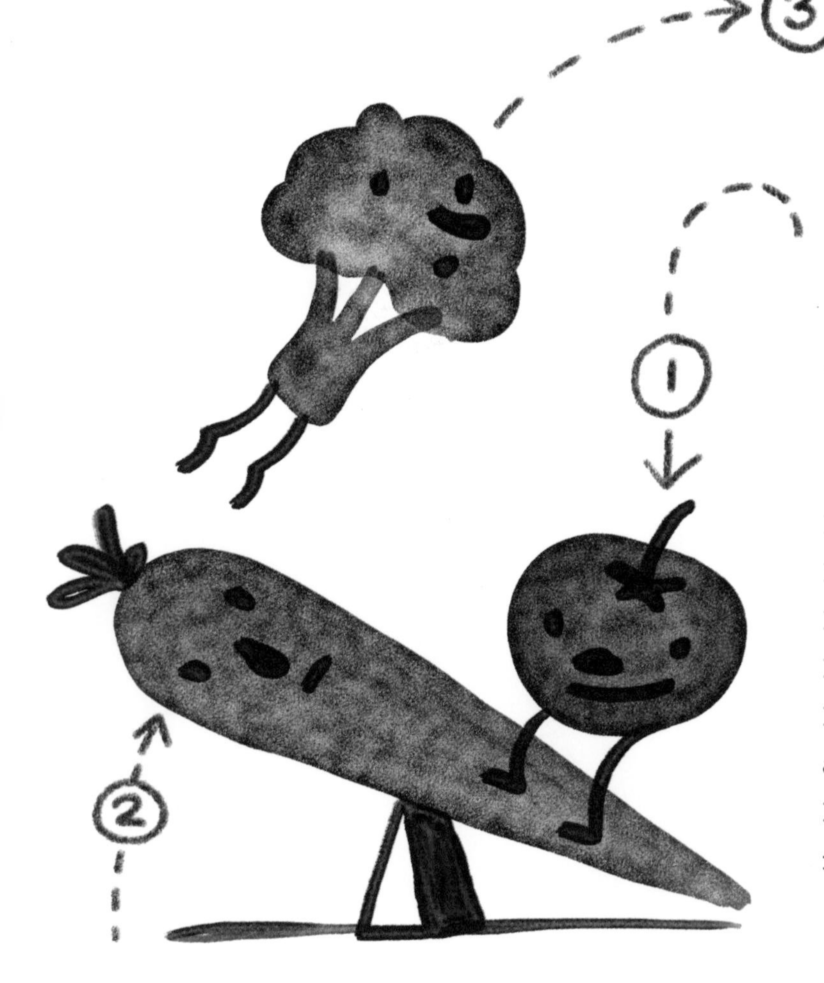


# Friends on the Menu

I'm gonna eat Henry.
I'm gonna eat Phil.
I'm gonna eat Debbie.
I'm gonna eat Jill.
I'm gonna eat Tommy
and Sue, no surprise.
Is it weird that I like to
name all my french fries?

*—Alan Katz*

# To Market, to Market

Mommy will squeeze a tomato,
An apple, peach and pear.
While I sit high in the grocery cart
And squeeze my teddy bear.

*—Diane Z. Shore*

# My Uncle Joe

My Uncle Joe came to our house
on Saturdays in leather.
He'd park his Harley on the curb
in ice-cold New York weather.

His cheeks, they glowed a ruddy hue,
my father's younger brother.
They both looked like my Grandpa Lou,
three versions of each other.

But Uncle Joe did wild things,
while Daddy just read fiction.
I loved it when he raced his wheels,
they made such red-hot friction.

And if I coaxed him long enough,
pleaded, begged and sighed,
my Uncle Joe would laugh and go
and take me for a ride!

*—Michele Krueger*

# Each Day at the Zoo Is Always New

Today I fed a giraffe at the zoo!
With green leaves clutched in my hand,
I reached
up
up
up
until I met a blue tongue
sweet eyes
funny horns
and a long, long, long neck.

Today I fed a giraffe at the zoo, but tomorrow
I might feed a kangaroo.

*—Margarita Engle*

# Lamb Said, "Mew"

Horse said, "Neigh."
Cow said, "Moo."
Dog said, "Woof."
Lamb said, "Mew."

Cat said, "Lamb,
This will not do.
Lambs say 'baa.'
Cats say 'mew.'"

Wren said, "Chirp."
Owl said, "Whoo."
Chick said, "Peep."
Lamb said, "Mew."

Cat said, "Lamb,
This will not do."
"I don't like 'baa,'"
Said Lamb. "Would you?"

Snake said, "Hiss."
Dove said, "Coo."
Hen said, "Cluck."
Lamb said, "Mew."

Cat said, "Lamb,
This will not do!
You must say 'baa'!"
Lamb said, "Mew!"

*—David L. Harrison*

# Our Kittens

One by one
our kittens found homes
till only one kitten had nowhere to go.

One by one
they all got new names,
new families, new blankets, new toys.

One by one
our kittens found homes
till only one kitten was left in the box.

One by one
they left purring in cars
snuggled in laps of new girls and boys.

One by one
we kissed them good-bye.
We waved as their cars drove them
far
far
away.

We felt happy and sad at the very same time.
And we let the last kitten stay.

*—Amy Ludwig VanDerwater*

# Running

I run with my dog,

jump-thump with my dog.

We race and both win

so we do it again.

He zigzags, I trip.

We tangle and slip.

We roll in the grass,

we get up and dash.

We flurry, we fly,

zap-flash through the sky.

We're the daisies, the bees,

we're the blue jays, the trees.

We're the shout in the sun

when my dog and I run.

*—Kate Coombs*

# All in a Day's Work

Picked an apple, chased a frog,

did my homework, pet a dog,

fed the goldfish, read a book,

played outside, learned to cook,

drew a picture, found a nest—

now, I guess, it's time to rest.

—*Timothy Tocher*

# The Dandelion

I caught a soft silk dandelion
gently in my hands
then blew a kiss
and secret wish
for when it came to land

On the wind I watched it soar
the dandelion that didn't roar
Across the trees and clear blue sky
it took my wish
and said good-bye

*—Mark Carthew*

# Wind

Leaf-stealer
Flag-flapper
Hat-snatcher
Branch-snapper

Sea-stirrer
Wave-whipper
Surf-raising
Sail-ripper

Door-slammer
Window-batterer
House-shaker
Peace-shatterer.

*—John Foster*

# A Hard Rain

Tonight the rain is falling hard.
It's washed the colors from our yard.
It's scrubbed the paint right off our house.
It's rinsed the fur right off a mouse.
The rain's turned fields to huge mud pies.
It's cleaned the stars up in the skies.
Rivers run and try to hide.
Tonight I think I'll stay inside.

*—Greg Pincus*

# Starry

Hey the starry nighttime
  and its starry plain,
starry is the silence
  of its starry train.
Starry are the curtains,
  starry wall and door,
starry falls the starlight
  on my starry floor.

Hey the starry nighttime
  and its starry glow,
starry is the window
  with the starry show.
Starry are the colors
  starry blue and red,
starry falls the starlight
  on my starry bed.

*—John Rice*

# Toasty, Warm Jammies

My toes
wiggle
into whispery, tappity footies.

My knees
hide
inside stretchy, squeezy legs.

My bum
dances
in the wiggly, waggly rump.

My arms
flap
in fleecy, fuzzy sleeves.

My belly
rounds
the long, skickety zipper.

My chin
taps
the cool, snippety snap.

Toasty, warm jammies
snuggle me
to drifty,
dreamy
sleep.

*—Lorie Ann Grover*

# Bedtime on 7th Avenue

Big old dog sighs and lies down.
Spider closes her many eyes.

In the vacant lot, weeds lean against
each other.

Even graffiti opens its loud neon mouth
and yawns.

*—Ron Koertge*

# Sleepless

"I don't feel sleepy," Lily whined.
"I can't turn off my busy mind.
My favorite show is on TV.
My best friend sent a text to me.
I have to study for a test.
I cannot sleep. I'm feeling stressed.
I need to floss. My mouth tastes yucky.
I have to find my rubber ducky.
My bedsheets don't smell clean tonight.
I think I felt a bedbug bite.
My room's too cold. Turn up the heat.
I need wool socks upon my feet.
You say the TV's broke tonight?
My cell phone isn't working right?
I'm feeling tired. Turn off the light."

*—Bruce Lansky*

# A Friend to the Rescue

Moon sinks.
No one remembered his birthday.
Just as he starts to fall
asleep and dream of next year,
Surprise!
Up pops Sun
like a cake ablaze
with 4.5 billion candles.
"Though really," says Sun,
"you don't look a day over
4.2 billion."
Moon beams.

—*Christine Heppermann*

# Gesundheit

A man knee-deep
In a field of hay
Sneezed so hard
He blew away.

As several people
Clapped and cheered,
He sneezed again
And reappeared.

*—David L. Harrison*

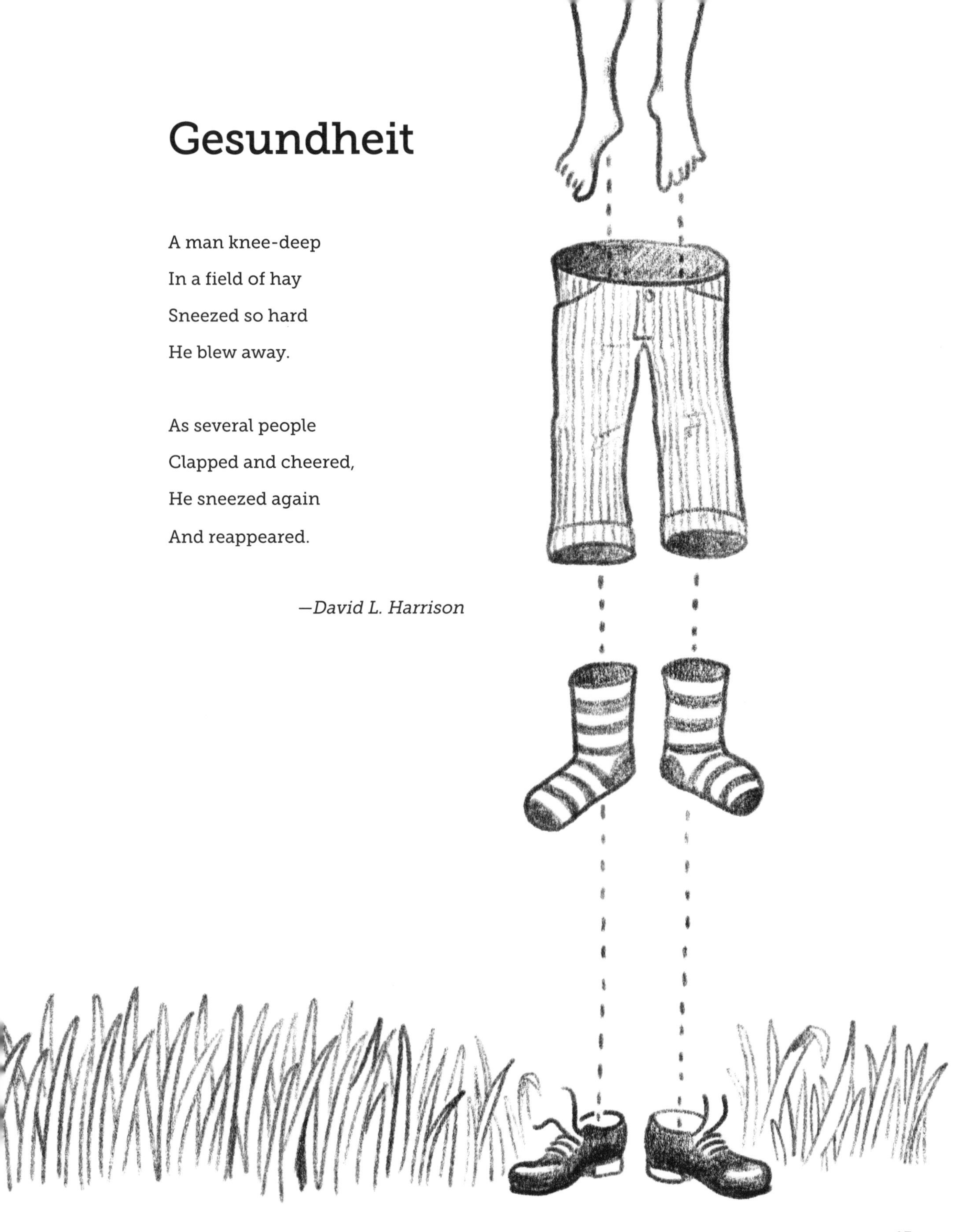

# An Odd Thing Happened...

O, last night an odd thing happened
When I had a little nap and
The wind blew off my cap and
It flew to Breezy Gap and
It landed on some chap and
I gave his arm a tap and
I said, "Hey, that's my cap!" and
He flew into a flap and
We had a little scrap and
His dog began to yap and
Attack my feet and snap and
I snatched back my old cap and
There came a thunderclap and...
I suddenly woke up!

*—Colin West*

# Have I Told You?

Ted, have I told you
you're cushy and cozy?
You're comfy to cuddle
and hold when I'm dozy.
I love how you nuzzle,
so fuzzy and snug.
There's no one I'd rather
have here for a hug.

So read me a page
and I'll read one to you.
We'll sing till we're sleepy
and then, when we're through,
we'll tuck in our covers,
we'll shut off the light,
and drift off to dreamland
together tonight.

*—Kenn Nesbitt*

# Bigger Than Big

It's bigger than big,
It's wider than wide,
It's deeper than deep
And there's nowhere to hide.

It lives in the bedroom,
It's close and it's snug,
It's coming to catch you,
Its name is—a hug!

*—Dennis Lee*

# Our Grandma Kissed a Pumpkin

Our grandma kissed a pumpkin
on a Friday afternoon.
She also kissed a crayon
and a giant red balloon.
I saw her kiss a chipmunk
eating cookies with a queen.
She kissed us in these costumes
at our house on Halloween!

*—Darren Sardelli*

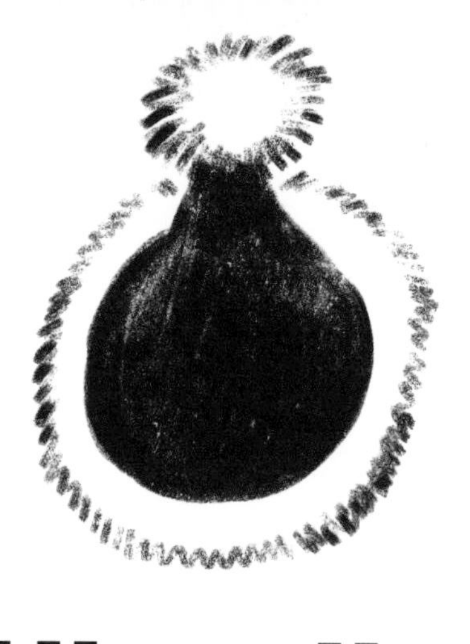

# I Have a Hat

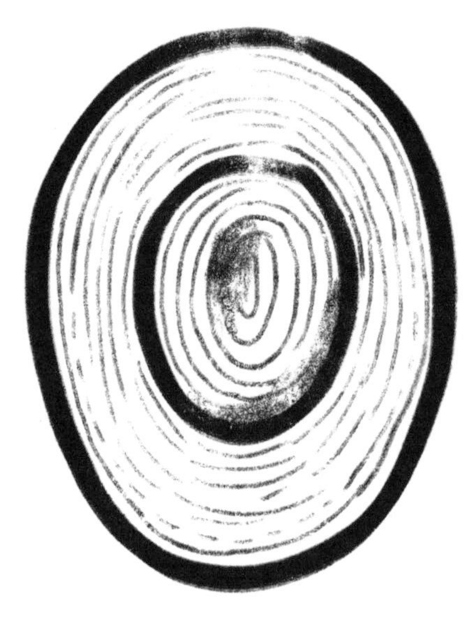

I have a hat to wear for church,
And one to wear for play.
There's one for when I throw a ball,
And one for everyday.

I have a hat that makes me sneeze,
With feathers waving tall.
My hat that's red and green and blue?
That hat's the best of all!

*—Verla Kay*

# Skateboard Girl

My dad sees my skateboard, uh-oh.

He commands, "Wear your helmet. Go slow."

But when I pop an ollie,

my dad cries, "Good golly!

Just look at my skateboard girl go."

*—B. J. Lee*

# The Tadpole Bowl

Summer means
the Tadpole Bowl,
up the street
from my cousins' house,
down concrete walls
where the rain collects,
after a desert storm.

Just us, just five,
bending between blades
of sharp tall grass,
scooping up handfuls
of cool wet mud,
thick and moving,
slick speckled tadpole heads
and tiny thin tails,
bump and tickle,
summer wriggles in our hands,
and then slips
through our fingers,
and disappears.

Soon our legs will grow,
and we will leap
into the world.

*—Libby Martinez*

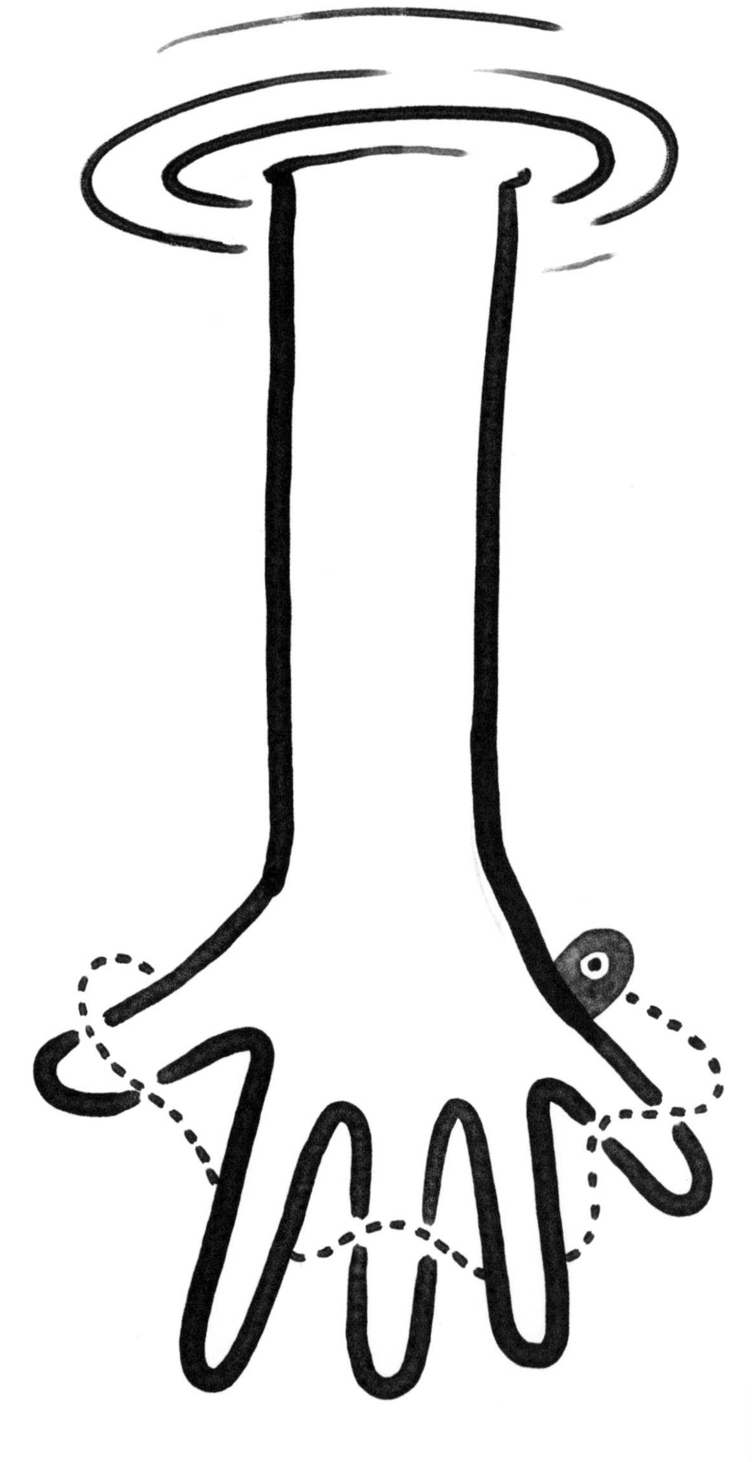

# Puppy Morning

Yip yip yip,
I'm here, I'm here,
so glad, so glad,
it's morning.

Thought thought thought,
the whole whole world,
had gone to sleep
forever.

*—Glenys Eskdale*

# School Bus

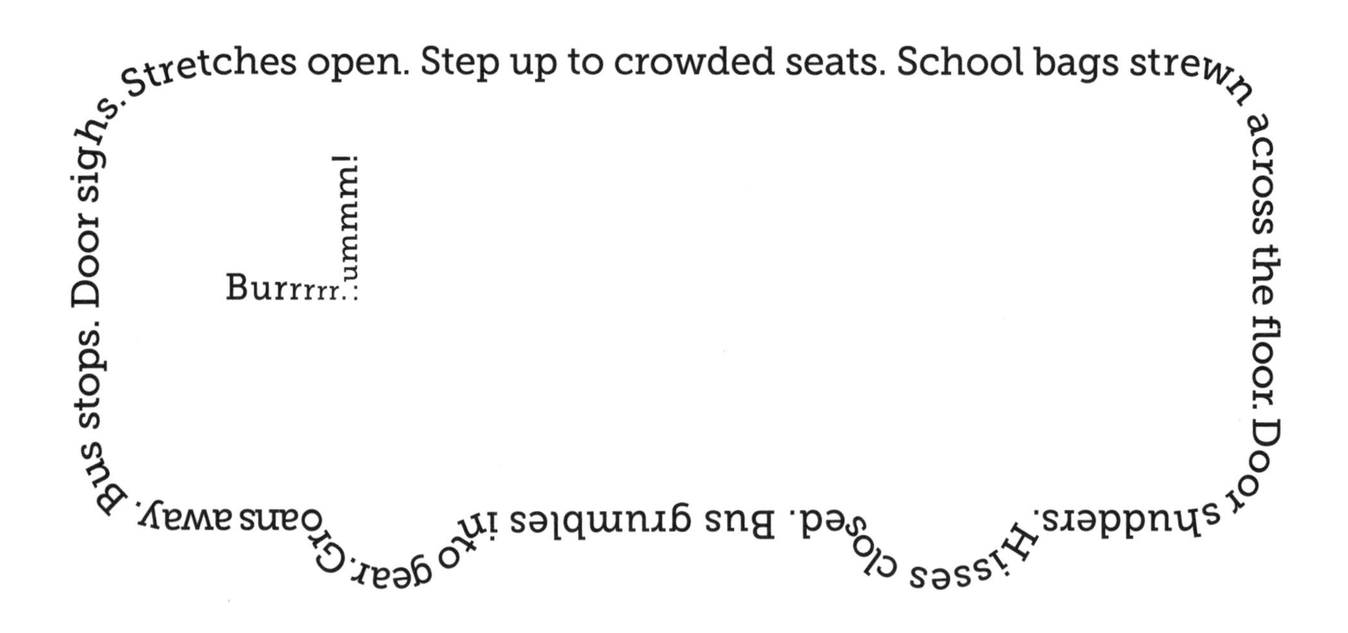


*—Kathryn Apel*

# First Day, Kindergarten

New dress
New hair
New shoes
New backpack
New school

Heart beats fast
Parents kiss bye

Cry
    A little

Walk
To new room
Sit
Sing
Play

    Block center
    Art center
    Science center
    Snack
Fun

First day, kindergarten
Done!

*—Sydra Mallery*

# Hummer

Quick

Quick

Quick

Flit

Flit

Flit

Flutter

Flutter

(SIP—SIP)

Flutter

Flutter

Flit

Flit

Flit

Disappear...

*—Jen Bryant*

# Seagull Beach Party

Dressed in their smartest white and gray,
The seagulls are having a party today.
All of the regulars are gathering here,
They've come from far, and come from near.
There's trim little Lightfoot, and beady-eyed Stumpy,
Lazy old Beaky, and squawky-voiced Grumpy,
Red Foot, and White Cap, and
Blackfeather Wing,
Watching to see what the humans will bring.

For seagulls love parties but never cook, ever,
Not starters or mains or dessert, or whatever!
They know it will come when the humans are here,
The menu will vary, of course, but no fear,
There will be lots to grip, gobble and take,
Bread crumbs and fries and, who knows, even cake!
And what you must do is to keep wide-awake
And never but never give another a break.
The fastest will win, but also the meanest,
A seagull party is never the cleanest!

*—Sophie Masson*

# An Orchestra in My Room

Flash!

Crack!

BOOOOOOOOOOOM!

My dog Jack hates thunder—
He shivers and quivers
And trembles and shakes,
Lies flat to the floor
Till the thunderstorm breaks.

Not me—
I jump into bed
Where it's cozy and warm
And snuggle in tight
Till the end of the storm.

I count all the flashes
And time every boom.
It's like there's an orchestra
here in my room.

Then down comes the rain—

Pitter
Patter
Spitter
Spatter
Splish
Splash
Splosh...

and I
slowly
drift
to sleep.

—*Meredith Costain*

# God Bless Me

God bless my daddy, God bless my mommy,
And the butcher who sells us hot dogs and salami.

God bless the fish in the tank and the sea,
God bless everyone. God bless me.

God bless the fireman up on the ladder
Who shows up to help when there's something the matter,

The gray kitty cat sitting high in the tree,
God bless everyone. God bless me.

God bless the library lady who shooshes,
The rabbit who's making his home in our bushes,

The weather guy living inside our TV,
God bless everyone. God bless me.

God bless the crossing guard out in the rain,
And all of those people way up in that plane,

The doctor who taps that one spot on my knee,
God bless everyone. God bless me.

God bless our neighbor who talks in Chinese,
God bless whoever invented grilled cheese,

God bless the dogs who can help people see,
God bless everyone. God bless me.

The bug lady who's at the nature museum,
The insects so small that you hardly can see 'em,

That shadow on bright, sunny days that I see,
God bless everyone. God bless me.

God bless my grandmas and grandpas and cousins,
Uncles and aunts and my friends by the dozens,

Everyone, everywhere, to infinity.
God bless everyone. God bless me.

*—Brian P. Cleary*

# River Song

Down by the river where the boats tie up
and the fishermen clean their catch
roll, river, roll
boats dip and rise on the slow turning tide
gulls flip and swoop like paper planes
blow, wind, blow
clouds roll and rumble in the darkening sky
the sun slides and hides behind a gray veil
boom, thunder, boom
rain pelts down and clatters on the water
ducks paddle in to the sheltering shore
rattle, rain, rattle
then clouds pass over like covers pulled back
the sun peeps out and shows a cheerful face
glimmer, sun, glimmer
the water smooths out, ripples lightly in the breeze
boats bob eagerly as the fishermen arrive,
carry tackle down the pier,
cast off ropes and raise their sails,
it's time to fish!
flow, river, flow...

*—Sherryl Clark*

# This Is the Hour

This is the hour
when dark hugs the stars,
and petals touch petals
to close up the flowers,

this is the hour
when songbirds alight,
feathers together
to share the quiet night,

this is the hour
when colors fade grays,
and only dark sparkles
rock by on the waves,

this is the hour,
moon magic above,
as I drift into dreams
I hear whispers of love.

*—Liz Brownlee*

# Sleepy

My eyes
are sleepy,
moonbeams fill
my head.

Kiss me
one more time.

Tuck me in
again
into
my
quiet
pillow-soft

time-for-dreaming
nighttime
bed.

*—Lee Bennett Hopkins*

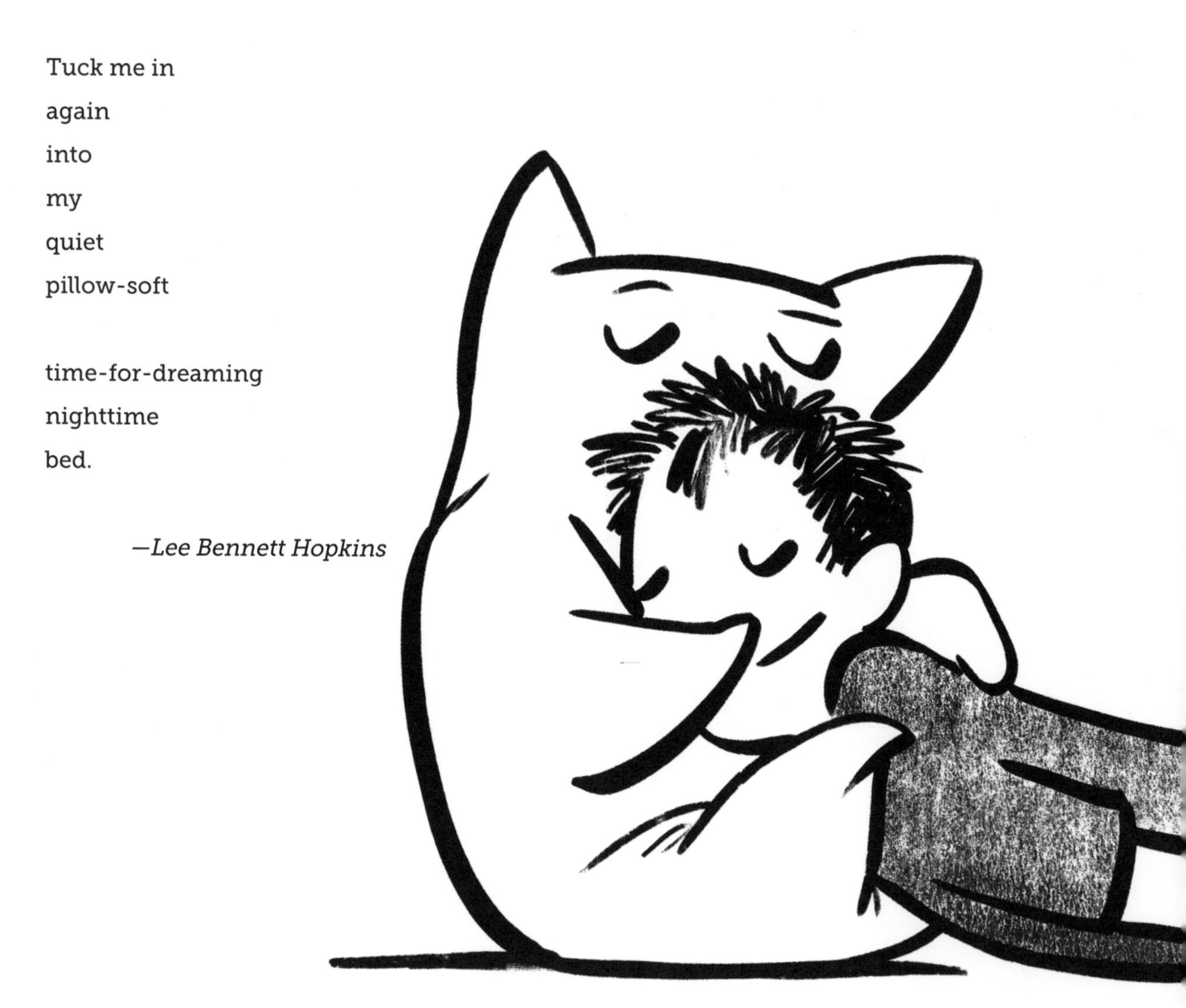

# It's Routine

Rose won't doze
until her toes
are snug in soccer socks.

My Aunt Louise
can't catch her Z's
unless she sets two clocks.

If the moon's too bright
Dad's up all night
counting leaping sheep.

Mom's pillowcase
of silk and lace
improves her beauty sleep.

Without his thumb
my brother's glum;
he won't slumber like a log
unless he nuzzles
—nose to muzzle—
his one-eared floppy dog.

We all hit the hay
in a different way.
Even mine gets funny looks.
I can't say good night
till tucked in tight—
with a blanket made of books!

*—Lee Wardlaw*

# The Seventeen Fitz Sisters

The seventeen Fitz sisters live in Bel-Air
and caused a commotion because of their hair.
There's nary a plumber who isn't aware;
the Fitz Sisters' Hair Clog was quite an affair.

Sixteen sisters showered one morning in May.
The seventeenth waited till later that day.
She turned on the faucet and found with dismay,
the drain wasn't draining, no how and no way.

Without getting angry or making a fuss,
she looked up the number for Plumbers R Us.
The phone was picked up by a plumber named Gus,
who asked if she had a clogged drain to discuss.

The first plumber promptly showed up at their door
in less than ten minutes, by quarter to four.
He brought plumbing gadgets and gizmos galore,
but sadly this obstacle called for much more.

The seventeen Fitz sisters looked on in fright.
Their hair was wedged into that drainpipe so tight,
it took twenty plumbers all day and all night
before they decided to use dynamite.

Imagine the horrible mess, if you dare.
Imagine the soap and shampoo everywhere.
Imagine the time that it took to repair!
Now imagine the Fitz sisters...all with short hair.

*—Andrea Perry*

# Three Bears Aboard an Iceberg

Three bears aboard an iceberg
that floated out to sea
(and quickly started melting)
were worried as can be.
Then one became the cargo
upon a tiny boat,
so one of them was rescued
but two remained afloat.

Two bears aboard an iceberg
went floating on adrift.
One said, "I hope a ferry
gives one of us a lift."
That's when they saw the sailboat
(the same one as before),
so one more bear was rescued...
which only left one more.

One bear aboard an iceberg—
a tiny block of ice—
sits searching for the sailboat
he's seen already twice.
He hopes and hopes the sailor
returns to rescue him
because, unlike the others,
he never learned to swim.

*—Samuel Kent*

# On Adopting a Pet Elephant

Pros:

Very helpful
Changing tires,
Cleaning gutters,
Dousing fires,
Saving cats,
Retrieving kites,
Throwing pitches,
Stringing lights.

Cons:

Should not jump.
Cannot skate.
Seesaw partner?
Not so great.
Tough to bathe
(a tad too wide).
Seeks quite well
But cannot hide.

Other considerations:

Doesn't bark or drool or shed.
Steals the covers.
Hogs the bed.

*—Linda Ashman*

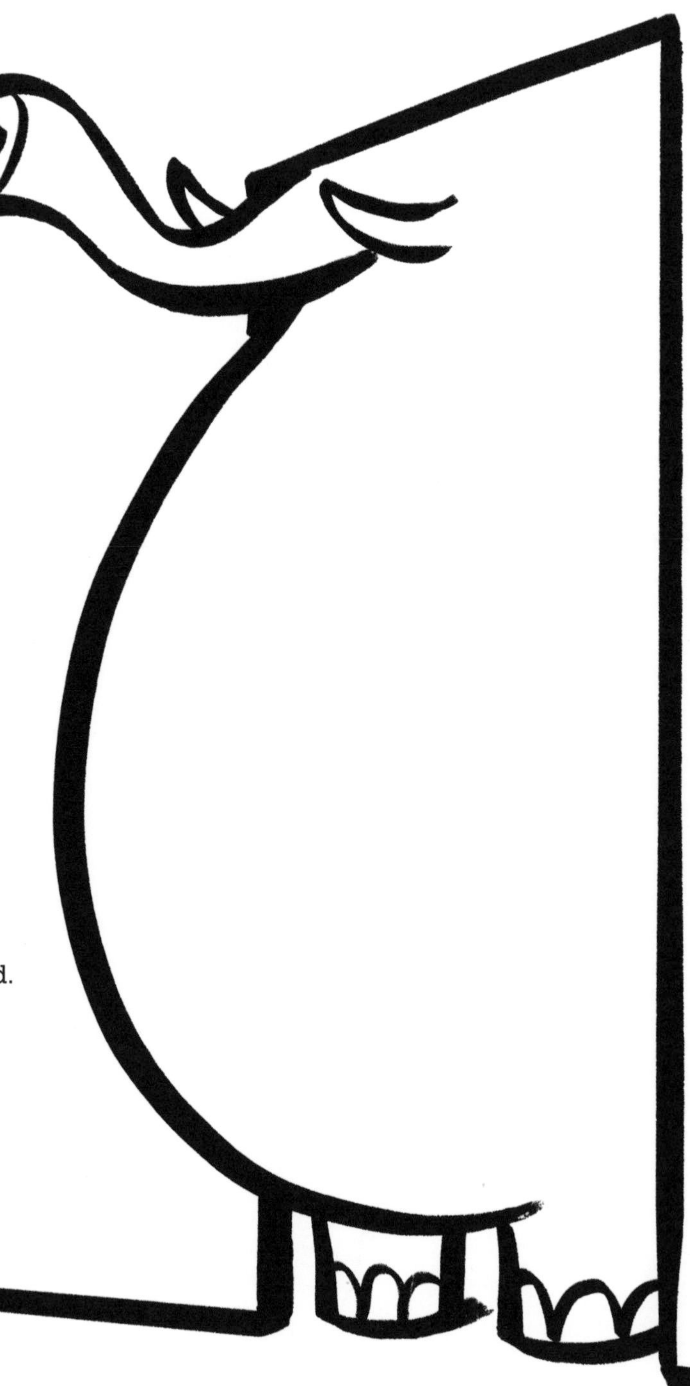

# What Do You Dream?

Teddy bear, teddy bear,
what do you dream?

*I dream of the salmon*
*that splash in the stream,*
*and fairy-tale forests*
*with towering trees,*
*and blueberry bushes*
*and honey from bees.*
*When you go to sleep*
*do you dream like I do?*

I dream of these poems
I'm reading with you.

*—Kenn Nesbitt*

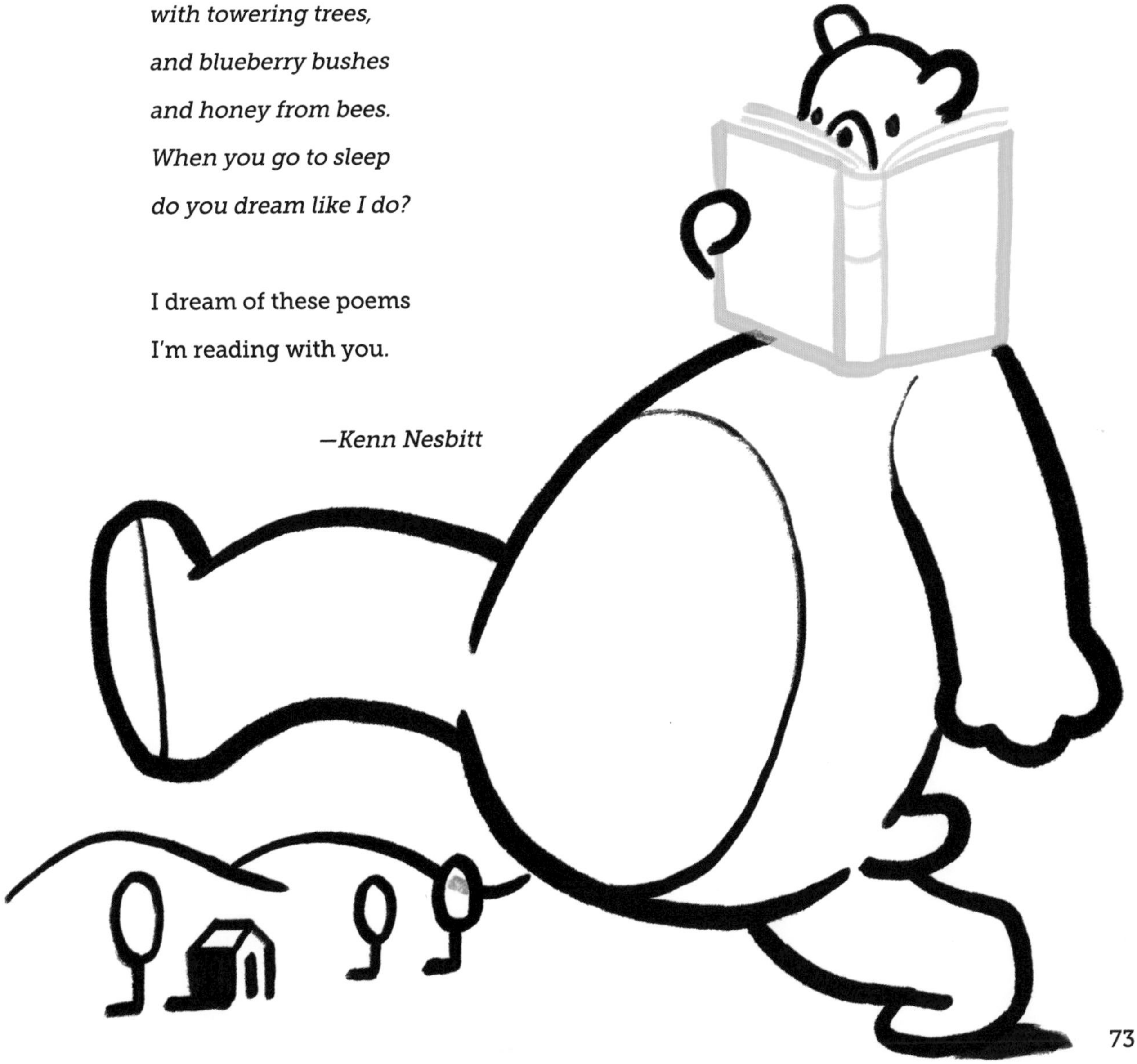

# Grandpa's Hair

There's hair growing out of his nostrils.
There's hair growing out of his ears.
There's hair in some places and wide-open spaces
where hair has been absent for years.

There's hair growing out of his knuckles.
There's hair on his pillow and bed.
There's hair in some places and wide-open spaces
but never a hair on his head.

*—Paul Orshoski*

# My Dad

My dad calls me Little Man.
He says we are *the Boys.*
He takes me to the shed with him
to get amongst his toys.
He tells me all about the tools
and what they're meant to do.
He even lets me loose with them...
He'll learn a thing or two!

My dad loves his helper,
I know for sure it's true–
That's why he shakes his head and asks,
"What will I do with you?!"
I help him with his messy jobs
and tag along behind...
I never know, when I'm with Dad,
what treasures I will find.

My dad is the greatest.
Oh the fun that we have had.
When I grow big and strong I'd like to be
*just like my dad!*

*—Kathryn Apel*

# Sleeping Over

I've been very busy, I've filled up my pack
with things I will need that will fit on my back.
There's Teddy and Wombat and Marmaduke Chook,
my football, my baseball, my animal book.
Now in goes my train set, the red signal box,
a few racing cars and my barrel of blocks.
I've got what I want and I'm letting them know
I'm sleeping at Grandma's and ready to go.

*—Celeste Walters*

# Rolling down the Hill

Sky,

grass,

sky,

grass,

Grandma,

grass,

grass.

*—April Halprin Wayland*

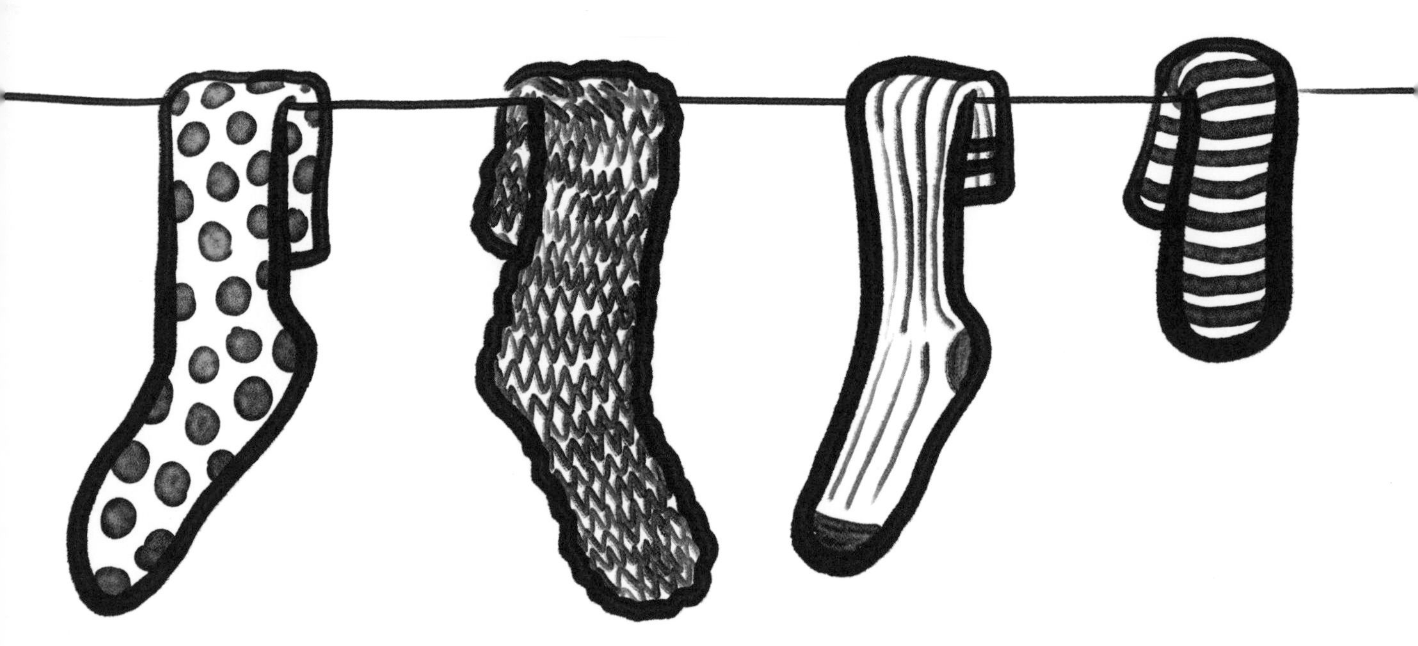

# Socks on the Washing Line

Socks in the washer,
Socks on the line,
Socks of yours and
Socks of mine:

Green socks, blue socks,
Old socks, new socks,
Yellow socks, red socks,
School socks, bed socks

Woolly socks, cotton socks,
Fluffy, pink, spotty socks,
Tired socks, gray socks,
Time-to-throw-away socks

Long socks, short socks,
Baby socks, sport socks,
Odd socks, posh socks,
Lost-in-the-wash socks

Socks of yours,
Socks of mine,
Socks in the washer and
Socks on the line.

*—Celia Warren*

# Me and My Feet

I like rain boots,
Purple shoes!
I like slippers
For a snooze.

I like dance taps,
But (you guessed!)
It is bare feet
I like best.

*—Donna Marie Merritt*

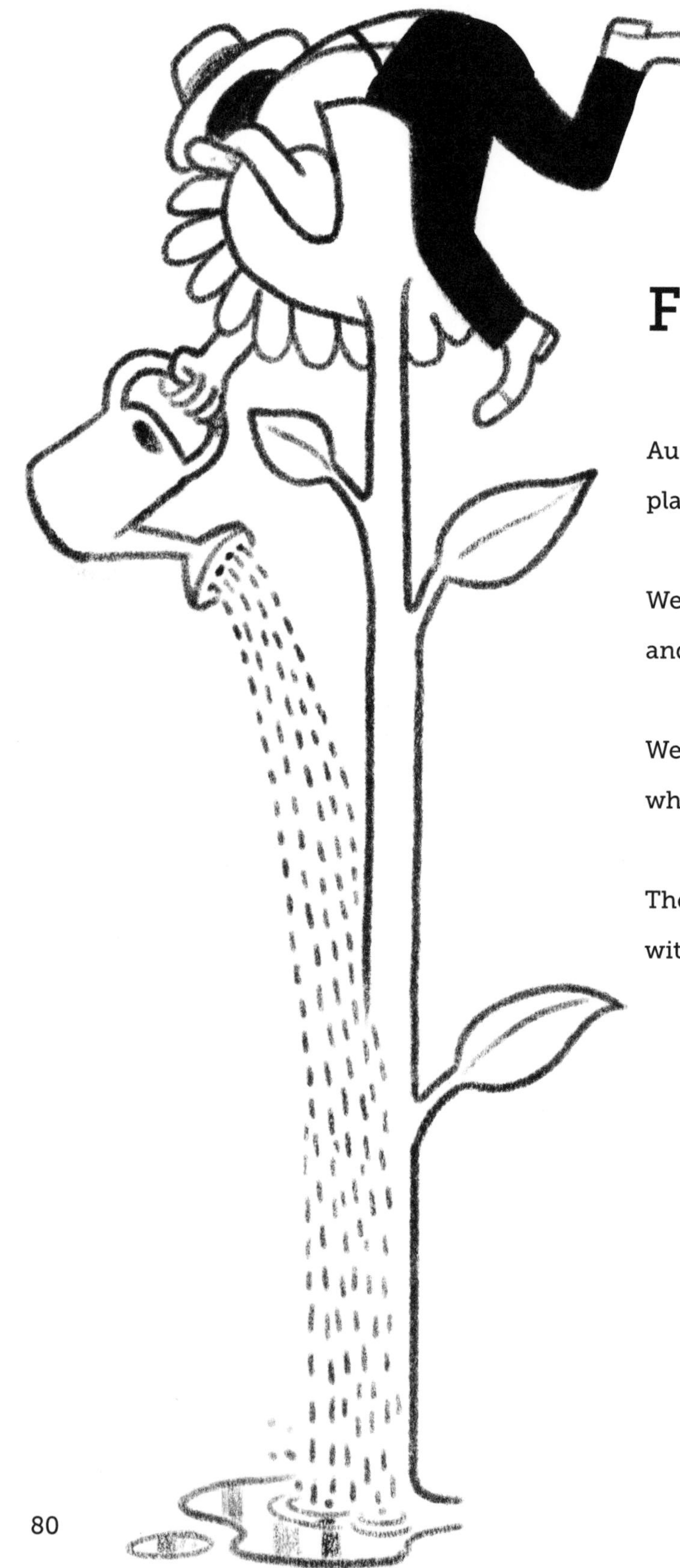

# Flower Power!

Aunt Sandra and I
plant sunflower seeds. *(Spring)*

We water the rows
and pull up the weeds. *(Summer)*

We harvest the seeds
when the season ends *(Autumn)*

Then share the seeds
with our feathered friends! *(Winter)*

*—Heidi Bee Roemer*

# Wild Flowers

Our dandelions

are tame, but their color is

a loud yellow roar.

*—Bob Raczka*

# Time to Sleep

Night has come.
Time to sleep.

Rooster dozes.
So does sheep.

Gosling settles in her nest.
Calf kneels in the field to rest.

Colt stands sleeping in his stall.
Horsefly slumbers on the wall.

Fox pup dreams inside his den.
Piglet snores inside a pen.

Gopher drowses in her hole.
So does woodchuck.
So does mole.

Baby duckling stops her peeping.
Baby spider ceases creeping.

Baby goat no longer bleats.
Baby bird no longer tweets.

Quiet now.
Snuggle deep.
Nighty-night.
Time to sleep.

*—Carole Gerber*

# Counting Rhyme

A ram
asleep,
a big-
horn sheep,
lies by
his lamb—
a steep-
hill two—

and soon
a ewe,
moon-white,
curls tight
against
a rock—

content
to be
a flock
of three.

*—Steven Withrow*

# Monkey Business

He puckers up his floppy lips
and waves his tongue about.
He comes up close, his hands on hips
and spits banana out.

He beats his little, chubby chest
with both his hairy arms
then flips himself and does his best
at walking on his palms.

He stands again and takes a bow
then climbs back up his tree.
It seems he's had enough for now
of imitating me.

*—Jenny Erlanger*

# A Visit to the Forest

Little squirrel climbs a tree,
stops to chew and chatter.
Cousin chipmunk runs away;
his feet go pitter-patter.

Bees are buzzing, flitting over
boysenberry flowers.
Garter snake goes sneaking under
tiny toadstool towers.

Ants are marching over pebbles,
working with no worries.
Sparrow sings and blue jay squawks;
a tiny rabbit scurries.

Watching all this hustle-bustle
nearly makes me dizzy–
I heard this was a pretty place,
but never knew how busy!

*—Matt Forrest Esenwine*

# Hippo

Hippo makes a bubbled yawn,
rolls over in her bed,
lets the water blanket her
and quilt around her head.
Slowly, lowly, she sinks deep
into a wet and soggy sleep.

*—Ann Whitford Paul*

# Baby's Bath Time

Huge heads
Thin tails
Mother elephants
On the trails.
Flapping ears
Keep them cool
Leading babies
To the pool.

Trunks like straws
To suck and blow
Squirt the water
High and low.
Baby elephants
Think it's fun
Having bath time
In the sun.

*—Brenda Williams*

# Boof

Boof's a made-up word I say.
I say it nearly every day.
It's very useful when I play,
And when I can't think what to say.

Boof works well for muttering,
For whispering and stuttering,
For bellowing and sputtering,
Boof's a useful uttering.

Boof is such a boofy boof.
It's good for boofing and for boof,
And when you want to boofly boof,
A boof can boofer quite a boof.

Boof is such a lovely word,
Although to some it sounds absurd.
Of all the words I ever heard,
I think boof's my favorite word.

*—Sonya Sones*

# Bath Time

A scrubbly, bubbly,
Rub-a-dub jumble.
A slippery, drippery slosh.
A muddle, a puddle,
A tumbly tuddle.
A jiggly, wriggly wash.

A splattery swish,
A splosh and a splish.
A drippy and flippery flash.
A bath full of bubble.
A tub full of trouble.
A wiggle, a giggle,
Kersplash!

*—Eric Ode*

# The Suit

Poppa has a footie suit.
He wears it down at work.
I know it seems a trifle odd,
but that's his only quirk.
His friends, at first,
were not impressed,
but then they followed suit.
Everybody wears them now.
Tourists think it's cute.

*—Calef Brown*

# PB Patty

They called her PB Patty for the
problem that she had.
Hooked on peanut butter,
PB Patty had it bad.

Creamy, crunchy, smooth, organic,
Patty ate it all.
She had a peanut butter poster
plastered on her wall.

For breakfast: peanut butter pancakes;
lunch: a PB shake.
Dinner was a peanut-butter-basted
T-bone steak.

"PB Patty," said her daddy,
"this has gone too far.
Your peanut butter passion has
become a bit bizarre."

He sent her to a doctor who could
cure her odd disease.
Four weeks later, she returned
as Patty Mac and Cheese!

*—Tiffany Strelitz Haber*

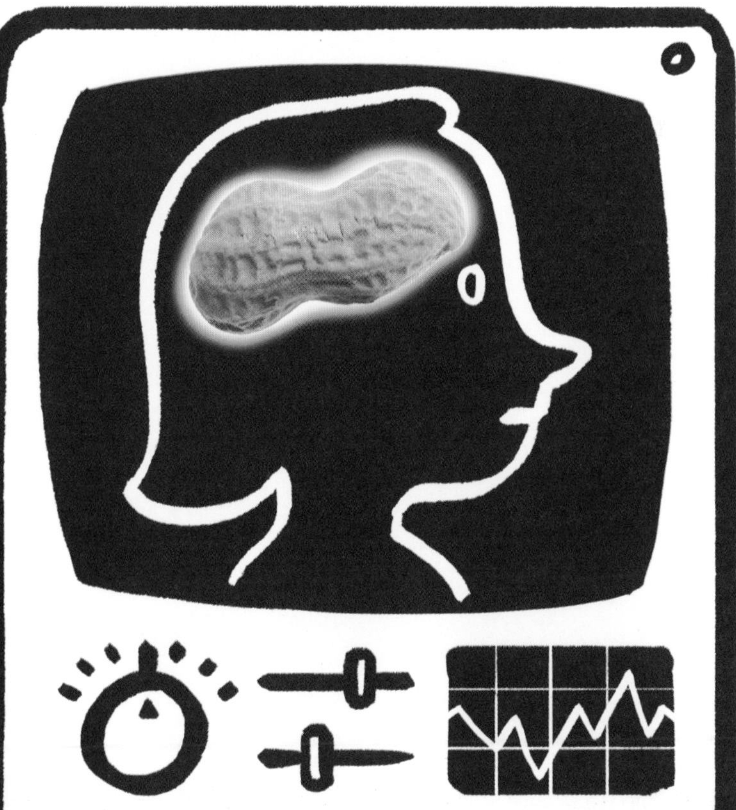

# Good-Night Poem

Now the long day
feels complete.

Tuck your feet
between clean sheets.

Tuck your body
into bed.

Tuck sweet dreams
into your head.

Tuck your covers
snug and tight.

Tuck the good
into the night.

—*Ralph Fletcher*

# Wiggle Wiggle

Wiggle fingers.
Wiggle toes.
Wiggle eyebrows
and your nose.

Wiggle elbows.
Wiggle head.
Wiggle belly
while in bed.

Wiggle pillow.
Wiggle feet.
Wiggle body
on your sheet.

Wiggle left and
wiggle right.
Wiggle down,
now say good night.

*—Robert Pottle*

# Ted, Ted, Climb in Bed

Ted, Ted,

climb in bed.

Grab that book

we've read and read.

Tuck the blanket.

Tuck the spread.

Here's a pillow

for your head.

Settle in.

Get ready, Ted.

Here come poems,

just ahead!

*—Kenn Nesbitt*

# The "Just Because" Hug

Bears will hug you 'cause they're mean,
so watch out for their claws!
But I don't hug you 'cause I'm nice.
I hug you just because.

There is no rule that says I must.
There are no hugging laws,
no hidden motives to discuss.
I hug you just because.

I do not hug you to reward
your virtues or your flaws.
Can you guess the reason why
I hug you? Just because.

When life's too busy, rushing by,
sometimes I like to pause
and wrap my arms around you. Why?
I hug you just because.

Just because I have two arms.
Be glad it's not two paws!
Just because it feels so good,
I hug you. Just because.

*—Robert Schechter*

# The Song of the Littlest Cat

*Chorus:*

Little Tinker Toy was a buttonhole cat,
And they don't get a whole lot smaller than that.
He wasn't really skinny, and he wasn't really fat,
And he went pitter-pat, pitter-pat, pat-pat.

1. He had a big room
And he had a big bed,
But he had a little pillow
For his wee little head.

2. And on his little head,
He wore a checkered cap
'Bout half as big around
As a gingersnap.

3. And on his little paws,
He wore buckle boots
And little red socks
With little green fruits.

4. And on his little legs,
He wore tight pants.
Well, he couldn't walk fast
But he sure could dance.

5. And on his little chin,
He grew a bit of fuzz
'Cause that's how big
Tinker Toy thought he was.

6. And on his little tail,
He wore a little ring
That he saved for the day
Of his wedding-ding.

*(Repeat chorus)*

1. Bed: Fold your hands together next to your face as if you are sleeping.
2. Cap: Pat-pat-pat the top of your head.
3. Paws: Hold one foot out and shake it.
4. Dance: Spin around, dancing in place.
5. Chin: Rub your hand on your fuzzy face.
6. Tail: Shake your rear end back and forth.

*—J. Patrick Lewis*

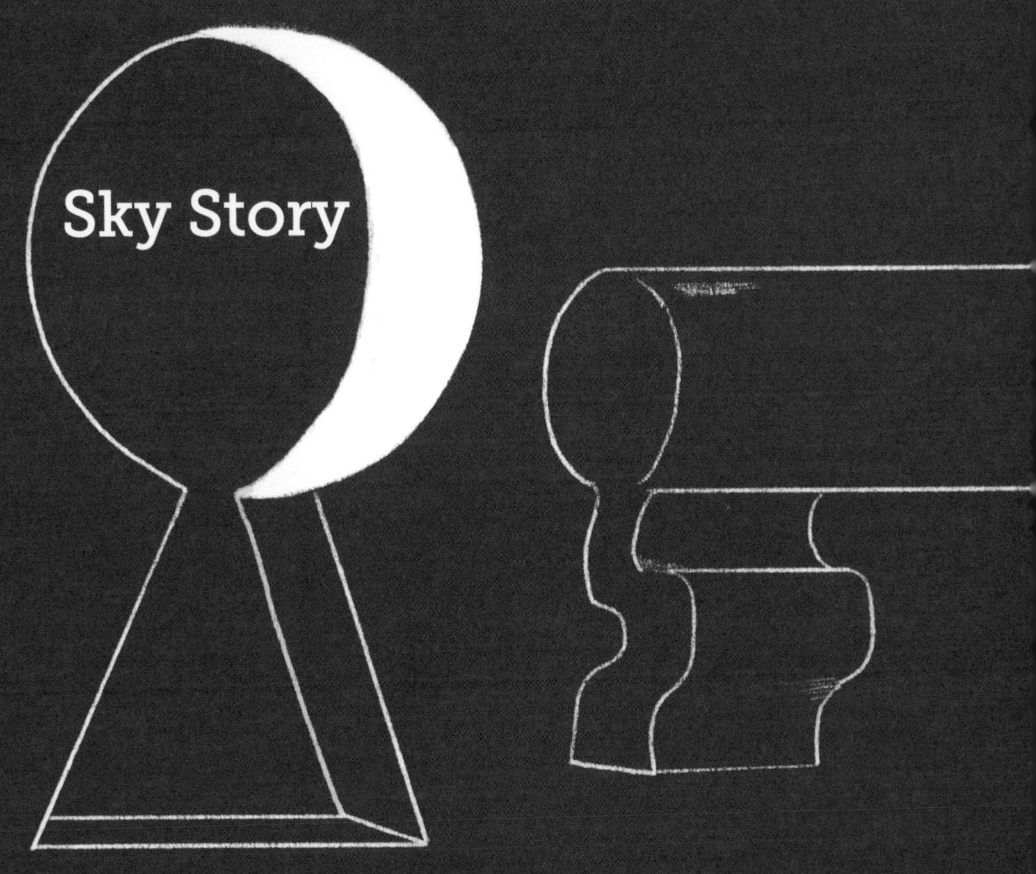

# Sky Story

Who has the keys
to the moon,
to the moon...
who has the keys
to the moon?
*Not me,*
said the owl,
said the owl;
*no keys.*
*Not me,*
said the mouse
as he nibbled his cheese.
*Not me,*
said the bee,
*Nor I,* said the fly.
*Only I,* said the sky.
*Only I.*

*—Rebecca Kai Dotlich*

# Happy Visits

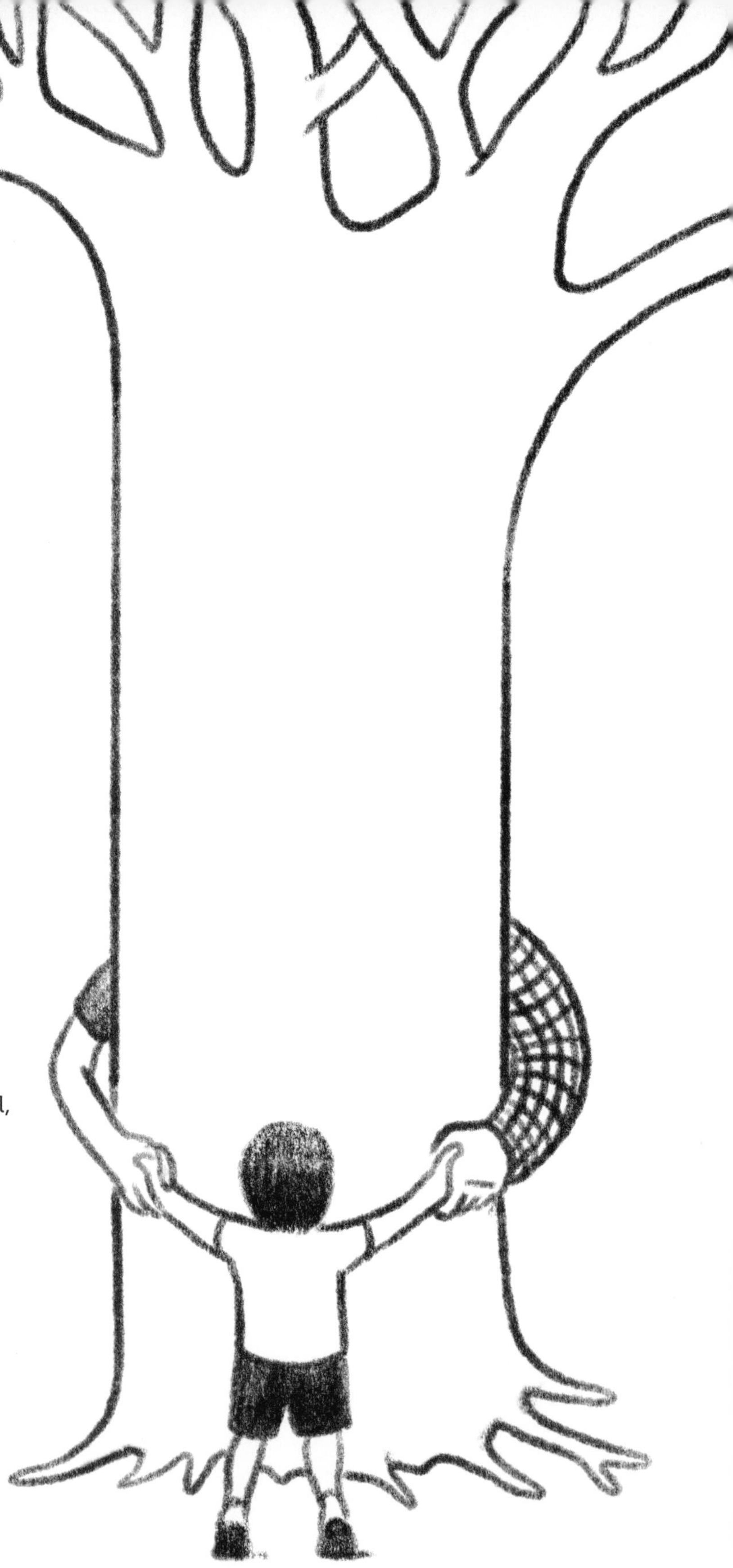

Lita and I like cookies,
Lita and I like tea.

Lito and I like whistling,
and inventing chocolate recipes.

The three of us like spying
a bunny hiding under a pine tree.

The three of us like watching
lizards and big, fat bumblebees.

I like to read us stories.
I sit in the middle of us three,

but best of all, best of all, best of all,
I like Lita and Lito to hug me!

We are the hugging three.

*—Pat Mora*

Lita—abbreviation of *abuelita*, "grandmother"

Lito—abbreviation of *abuelito*, "grandfather"

# We're Bats

Our wings are leathery
Sheets of stretch
We carve the sky

At night we etch
A trail through twilight
Chasing gnats

We swoop
We dive
We fly

We're bats

*—Laura Purdie Salas*

# Crickets

Chirping in the dark, their song

Resonates

In the still air. A

Chorus of summer night strummers in concert with

Katydids

Entertaining warm evenings with

Their

Symphony of wings.

*—Elaine Magliaro*

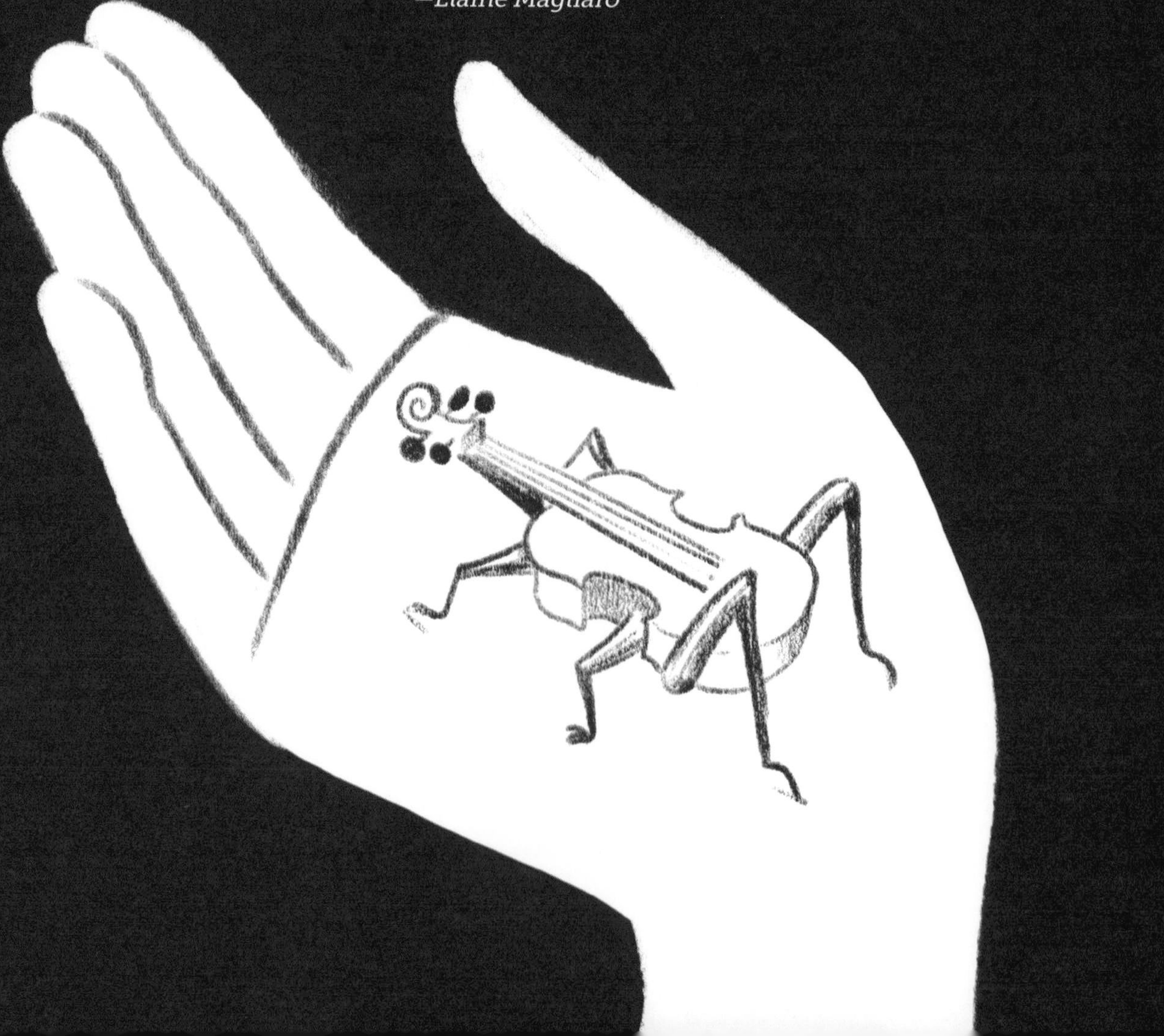

# Rainbow

The watery sky
rings herself dry,
and leaves us a gift
to remember her by.

*—Betsy R. Rosenthal*

# Tasty Moon

In Heaven's oven
the moon is a chunky pie
  sugarcoated and crusty,
  as plump as a doughnut,
  as dimpled as a dumpling—
Good enough to eat.

*—Dianne Bates*

# The Banquet of the Sun

Now the stars shake their fine grains of light.
Now the golden door yawns, the oven opens,
and light spreads on the platter, frosting the dark
with the slow syrup of light waking.

Out of the oven of darkness
silently something stirs and stirs it.
The sun is ready! Orange and gold.
Help yourselves. There is enough for all.

*—Nancy Willard*

# Tuck a Poem in Your Head

At night before
you go to bed,
tuck a poem
in your head.

Hold it softly
as you sleep,
twist it, turn it,
try to keep

its rhythm rumbling
deep, so deep,
just beyond
the edge of sleep.

Dance with it the
whole night through,
and when the day
comes back to you,

boldly bouncing
on your bed—
blink your eyes
and shake your head.

See if now
a poem slips…
from your
newly wakened lips.

*—Joan Bransfield Graham*

# The Little Red Bed

I'm spending the night in my own little bed.
It fits me just right, and it's fire-engine red.
  A blanket for my body.
  A pillow for my head.
Just me and my dreams in my very own bed.

Although when I'm eating, I still wear a bib,
I'm big enough now that I don't need a crib.
  I don't need Mom or Daddy.
  I sleep alone instead.
Just me and my dreams in my very own bed.

So read me a book now. Then turn out the light.
Tell me you love me, and kiss me good night.
  Sing to me softly
  and tuck me in tight.
Just me and the night and my very own bed.

Just me and my dreams in my bed.

—*Allan Wolf*

# When Daddy Tucks Me In

The sea is still,
the wind is warm,
there is no rain,
there is no storm,
there is no need
to be forlorn
when Daddy tucks me in.

The grass is green,
the clouds are white,
the trees are lush,
the sky is bright,
there's no such thing
as darkest night
when Daddy tucks me in.

There is no fog,
there is no gloom,
the bunnies hop,
the flowers bloom,
the sun starts shining
in my room
when Daddy tucks me in.

The heavens laugh,
the angels sing.
I've one complaint,
just one small thing—
the bristles on
his hairy chin,
when Daddy tucks me in!

*—Joshua Seigal*

# Little Hand

Little hand,
open wide,
put a special kiss inside.
Save it for a rainy day
or say bye-bye,
blow it away.

*—Michelle Heidenrich Barnes*

# Adventures in Slumberland

I fell asleep while reading *Goodnight Moon*
And dreamed I got to hold the red balloon.
Its string was tightly gripped within my hand;
It floated over me in slumberland.
It pulled me up—it felt like we could fly,
And so we did, my red balloon and I.
The ceiling of my bedroom opened wide
And up we went to see the things outside.
I looked below and saw my climbing tree;
For once, it didn't look that big to me.
And then my schoolyard, full of kids, appeared;
I think I might've seen myself (that's weird!).
I saw the playground bully. He looked small.
I thought, *He doesn't look that tough at all!*
There's Grandma's house—it's closer than I thought!
Hey, I should visit (she'd like that a lot).
It's strange: Though things look small as up we soar,
The moon looks so much bigger than before!
Next morning, *Goodnight Moon* was on my bed
And such amazing thoughts were in my head.
So many things are different than they seem
And oh what fun to fall asleep and dream.

*—Chris Cook*

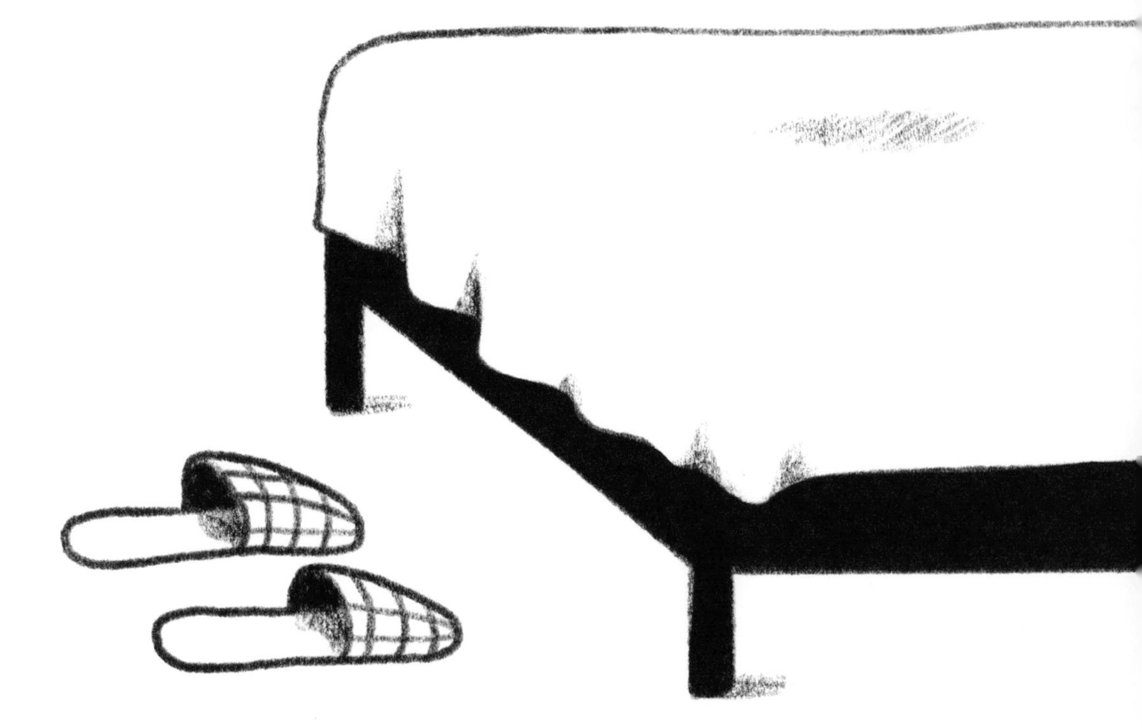

# Oliver's One-Man Band

Oliver Oscar Octopus
Is stirring the sea and the sand
Ollie plays all of the instruments
In Oliver's One-Man Band

Oliver's tooting a tuba
And crashing away on his drum
Oliver's plucking a banjo
As all of his lobster friends hum

Oliver bashes the cymbals
While sawing the violin strings
It sounds like a heavenly choir
When Ollie the Octopus sings

This song's his famous finale,
A tune called "The Tuna Got
Canned"
Now there's a rousing ovation
As Ollie's eight arms get a hand!

*—Jeff Mondak*

# The Fur-Bearing Trout

Have I told you about the fur-bearing trout,
with hair growing over its back?
You never could wish for a woollier fish,
hirsute as a raggedy yak.

Magnificent braids? It has them in spades!
They grow from its neck at the nape.
It is quite debonair in its swaddle of hair
a bit like a carp, with a cape.

It swims back and forth in the lakes of the north,
where the water in winter will freeze.
As other fish shiver their gills in the river,
the fur-bearing trout is at ease.

It wraps itself tight in its hair for the night,
and sleeps, drifting hither and yon,
in the shade of a ship, as it dreams of a trip
to a stylish, aquatic salon.

*—Robert Paul Weston*

# Octopus

Shape-shifter
rock lifter
clever drifter
          octopusssssss
master blender
cave defender
what's your gender?
          octopusssssss
big eye winking
always thinking
slowly sinking
          octopusssssss
color-mixer
inky fixer
slinky trickster
          octopusssssss

but not like us
          octopusssssss

*—Harry Laing*

# What to Yell When You're Trapped in the Belly of a Whale

Help! Help! Help!

Help! Help!

Help!

Help!

Help!

Help!

Help!

Help!

Help!

Help! Help! Help! Help! Help! Help!

Help! Help! Help! Help! Help! Help!

Help! Help! Help! Help! Help! Help!

Help! Help! Help! Help! Help!

Help! Help! Help! Help! Help!

Help! Help! Help! Help! Help! Help!

*—James Carter*

# Say Good Night

Before our mom
turns off the light,
let's take some time
to say good night
to everything
and everyone.
Good night to sky.
Good night to sun.
Good night to Mommy.
Daddy too.
Good night to me.
Good night to you.
Good night, starlight.
Good night, moonbeams.
Good night, sleep tight.
Good night, sweet dreams.

*—Kenn Nesbitt*

# Playmate

All alone on a sunny day?
You have a friend who wants to play!
Yes, that's the time you have a chance
to take your shadow out to dance.
Swing your arms around & around.
Your shadow's arms swing on the ground.
Make curves & circles, angles, too.
Your shadow does just what you do.
Crouch down!
          Jump up!
                    Left, right
                              Legs KICK!
Your shadow knows your every trick.
But should there be a cloudy day,
your shadow simply slips away.

*—Bobbi Katz*

## me

I was once so very small

I hardly knew me, not at all.

But in a mirror I could see

that there I was...

and I was me!

*—Janeen Brian*

# Dear Tooth Fairy,

My name is Harry.
I lost my front tooth,
but to tell you the truth,
I swallowed it whole
in a cinnamon roll.
So there's nothing beneath
my pillow, no teeth.
I've nothing to trade
but this drawing I've made.
I hope you'll be kind?

Sincerely signed,
Your toothless friend

(The End.)

*—Julia Durango*

# My Blankie

Got a blankie,
Old and manky.
Sometimes use it
As a hanky.
Gray-y pinky,
Smudgy, inky,
Battered, tattered,
Rather stinky.
Sucked and chewed
And glitter-glued
And covered in
All kinds of food.

Good to cuddle,
Dropped in puddle.
In the toy box
(What a muddle!).
*Now* where is it?
Let me see.
Where on earth
Could blankie be?
Wash it? Dry it?
Guess that's fine.
But take it? NO!
THIS BLANKIE'S MINE!

*—Elli Woollard*

# I Can't Sleep When It's Hot

So
my Korean grandmother, my *halmoni*,
brings me a big long hollow pillow
woven from strips of bamboo.
She says it's called a *jukbuin*,
which means "bamboo wife."
I snuggle up and hug it
and it makes me feel cool.
"But, Halmoni," I say,
"I'm too young to be married!"

*—Janet Wong*

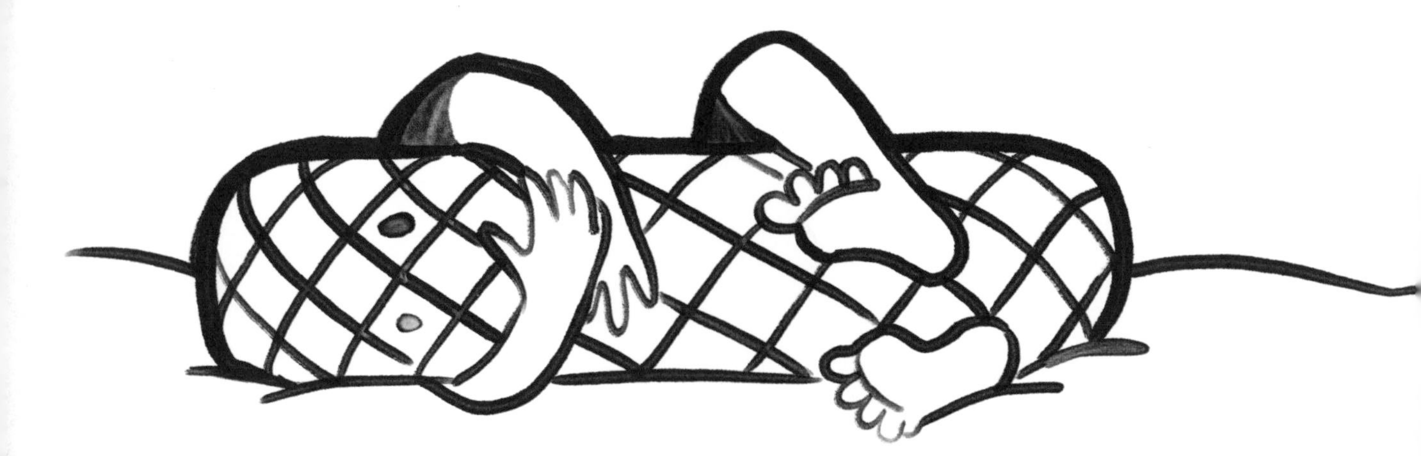

# Mama and Papa

We hide our nest high in a cedar tree.
We line it with feathers and fluff.
We keep our eggs warm for eleven days,
and when we've waited long enough,
five baby birds crack open their shells,
scramble out and open their beaks.
In and out of the nest we fly,
feeding our babies for two long weeks.
They eat and grow. They grow and eat.
They grow too big for the nest.
They flap their wings.
          They try.
                    They fly!
Now can we get some rest?

*—Helen Frost*

# Duckling Day

Bouncing, bobbing through the rushes,
where it's green and dim,
ducklings on their first day out go
bouncing, bobbing. Swim!
Gliding, sliding, water snake slips,
hungry for a snack.
Mama duck knows what to do—
make racket! Quacket-quack!
Wings flap, bill snaps—such a quacking
Mama duck can make!
So much racket! Too much quacket!
Off goes water snake.
Ducklings bounce and ducklings bob
through rushes green and dim.
First day out and safe with Mama,
baby ducklings swim.

*—Cynthia Porter*

# Shelter

Such a slim space you're tucked into,
Butterfly:
feet
stuck to
the underside
of this dripping leaf,
wings shut tight like a
flat gray purse holding
ribbons of color.

*—Joyce Sidman*

# Baseball Season

Batter up!
Take your stance.
Watch the pitcher do his dance.

Swing the bat—
hit or miss,
innings go along like this.

Hit the ball,
run the bases.
See the smiles on teammates' faces.

Slide in safe
at home plate—
this is when baseball is great!

*—Kelly Ramsdell Fineman*

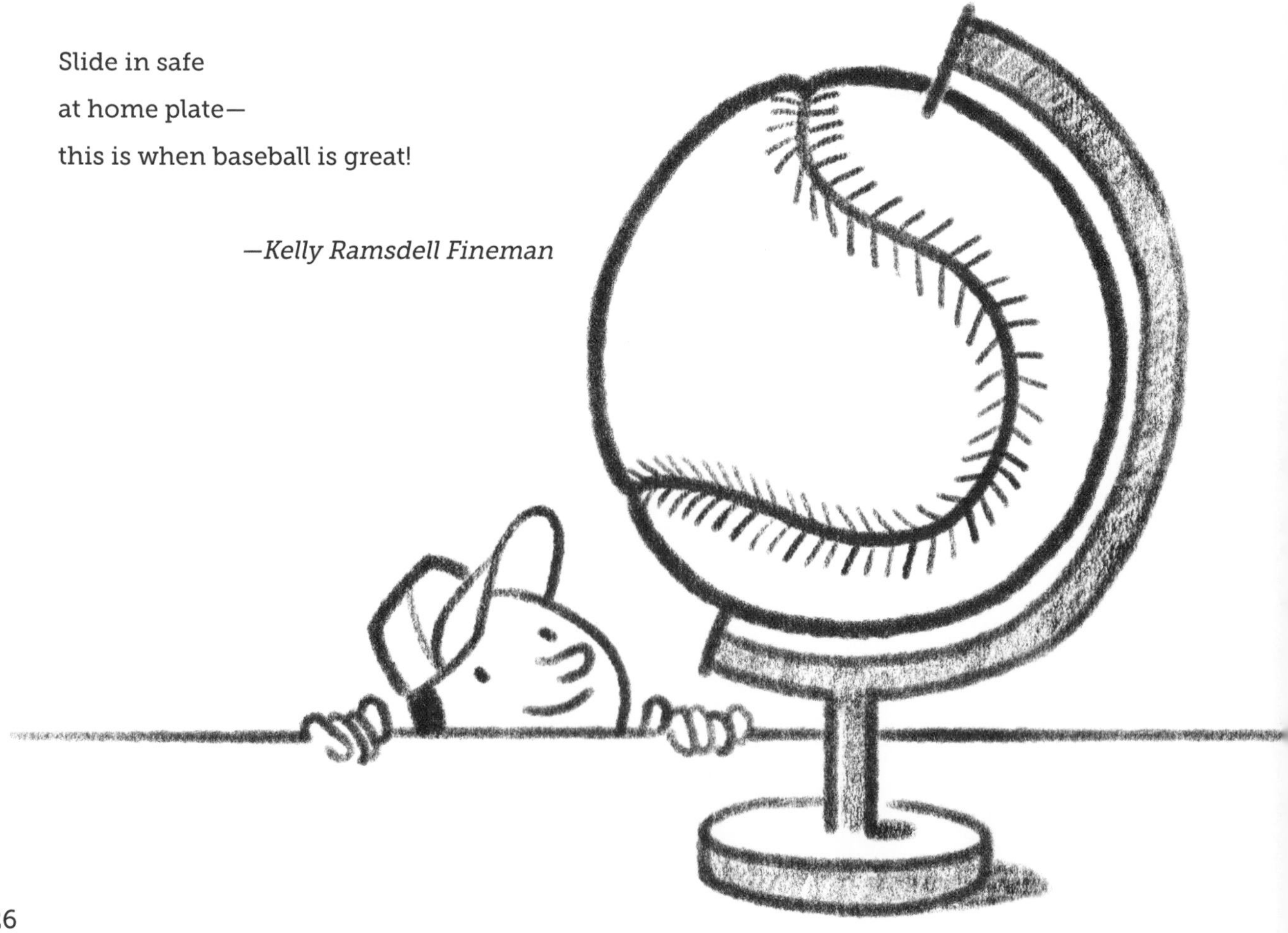

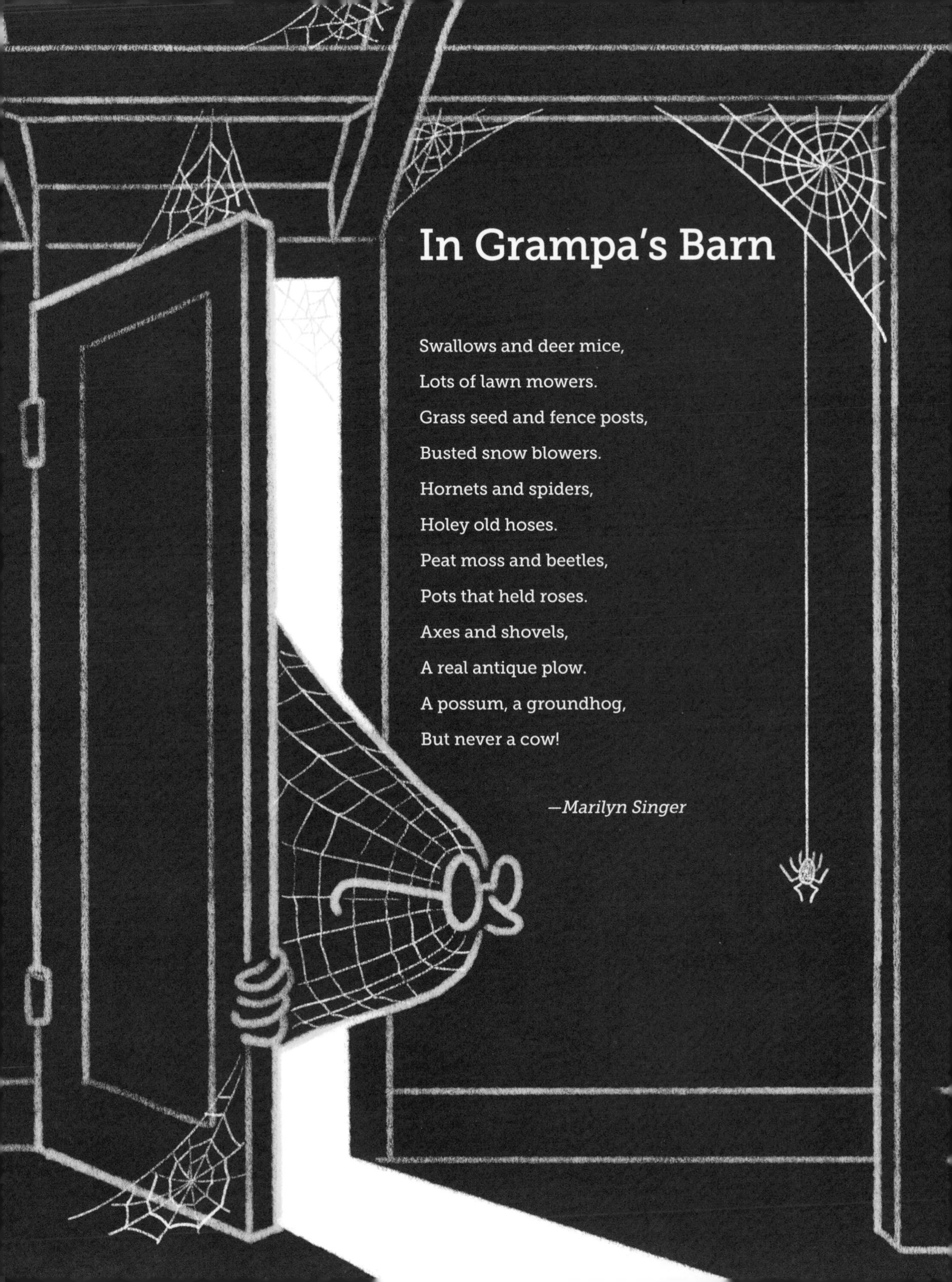

# In Grampa's Barn

Swallows and deer mice,
Lots of lawn mowers.
Grass seed and fence posts,
Busted snow blowers.
Hornets and spiders,
Holey old hoses.
Peat moss and beetles,
Pots that held roses.
Axes and shovels,
A real antique plow.
A possum, a groundhog,
But never a cow!

*—Marilyn Singer*

# November Volcano

November volcano

exploding

a lava of leaves

—*Heidi Mordhorst*

# September

New shoes and school supplies—
Chestnuts dropping brown buttons down
The long skirt of the lawn.
And the first frost, sharp
As the scratch of a kitten.

*—Liz Rosenberg*

# Years

It's fall and all the leaves are falling.

Winter winter winter's calling.

Say good-bye to bicycles.

Say hello to icicles.

Round and round the seasons go.

Spring waits under winter's snow.

Seasons come and seasons go.

*What a lovely thing to know.*

—*Mary Ann Hoberman*

# Tracks

small animal tracks
quilt the white blanket of snow
with uneven stitches

—*Tracie Vaughn*

# Jerry's Snowman

I wonder

how the artist felt,

when his art

began to melt.

*—Kalli Dakos*

# Snow Angels

Together,
we lie in the snow.

Peaceful angels,
moving slow.

Making wings,
arms spread wide.

Flapping gently
side by side.

—*Carole Gerber*

# Bedtime

Smoochie, smoochie,
kissie, kissie—
lovey-o brother, lovey-o sissie,
huggie-o, hug, hug,
into pajama,
lovey-o daddy, lovey-o mama,
lovey-o kitty,
lovey-o pup,
love up-downy-o, love downy-up...
tickle-in-the-rib time,
lovey-o teasy,
bit more lovey-o, bit more squeezy,
Love, love, lovey-o,
time for bed—
oh, my aching lovey-o head.

*—Julie Larios*

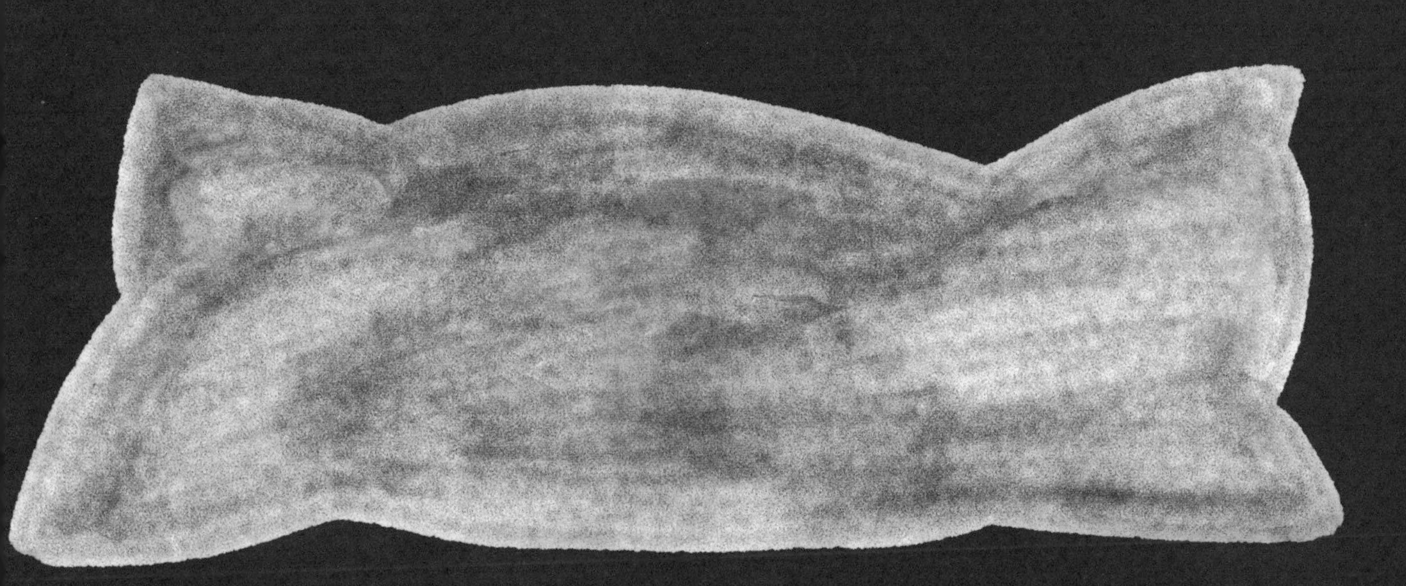

# Bed, Sweet Bed

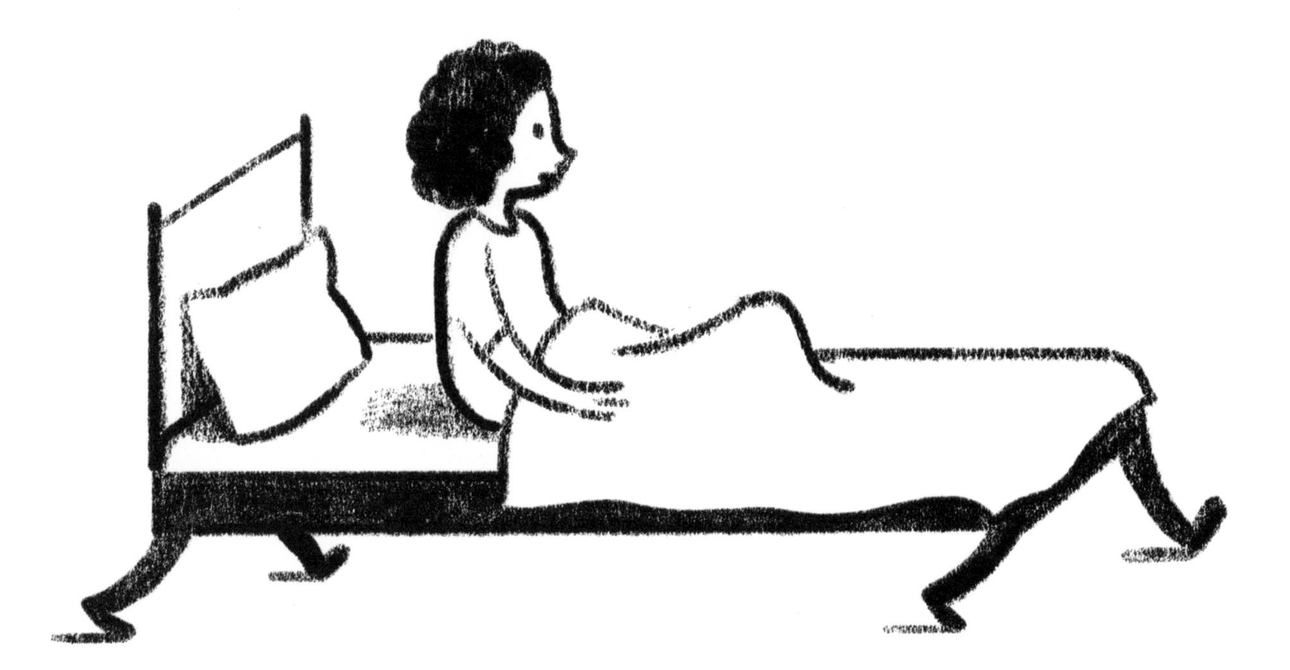

Of all the magic places
In all the tales I've read,
Not one is more enchanting
Than my humble little bed!

My bed's not just for sleeping
Or hiding from my chores.
My bed's a mighty fortress
For fighting dinosaurs!

My bed's a rocket launcher
That shoots me into space.
My bed's a roaring stock car
That helps me win the race.

My bed's a three-ring circus
Where I do flips and bends.
My bed's a puppy clinic
For treating furry friends.

And even when I'm sleeping
Until tomorrow morn,
My bed is still amazing—
It's where my dreams are born!

—*Brian Rock*

# Q+U

If I could do anything at all

You know what I would do?

I'd turn into a letter,

Specifically a *Q*.

That way I'd spend every day

Right there next to *U*.

And *U* would be my love

Because it's *U* whom I would woo.

(By *I*, of course I mean *Q*. I, *Q*, don't mean to confuse you, *U*.)

—*Joe Mohr*

# Count Your Blessing

Be grateful for your hat,
It means you likely have a head.
Don't worry if you don't,
It's as likely then you're dead.

*—Lemony Snicket*

# The World's Longest Yawn

Verity Vaughn did the world's longest yawn.
It lasted for seventeen weeks.
She walked round outside
With her mouth open wide
Showing off the insides of her cheeks.

While her mouth was ajar (as most yawning mouths are)
Several flies flew around to explore.
A mouse tried to follow,
But Verity swallowed
And the mouse and the flies were no more.

A cat looked inside for a good place to hide
From a dastardly dog called Big Dave.
But he didn't stay long,
For a bear, big and strong,
Mistook Verity's mouth for a cave.

When her yawn finally ended her friends thought her splendid
And gave her a round of applause.
But the grizzly bear
Is still resting in there
Fast asleep between Verity's jaws.

—*Mike Lucas*

# How to Fall Asleep

Hey, Ted, in just a little bit,
we'll need to go to sleep.
So let me show you how.
It's far more fun than counting sheep.

Lie down in bed and close your eyes.
Now take a breath and sigh,
and picture you're an airplane and you're
flying through the sky.

Now fly a little lower through
the clouds and in the breeze,
until you see the water of
the slowly rolling seas.

Then settle on the water where
you've now become a boat,
and feel the ocean rock you
gently, gently as you float.

Now turn into a submarine
and sink beneath the waves,
to watch the fish swim in and out
of underwater caves.

You follow them inside,
exploring tunnels as you go.
It's quiet here, and everything
is beautiful and slow.

So you become the water now,
and you become the caves,
and you become the ocean and
the gently rocking waves.

It's peaceful on the ocean bed,
so silent, warm, and deep,
so spread yourself across the world
and drift away to sleep.

—*Kenn Nesbitt*

# Gran's Visit

Gran took me to the beach today.
The water washed my toes.
But when I felt a little scared
Gran smiled and kissed my nose.

Gran took me to the park today
And we played hide-and-seek.
But when I cried 'cause I felt lost
Gran smiled and kissed my cheek.

Gran had to pack her bag today
To go back to her place.
So when she looked a little sad
I smiled and kissed her face.

*—Sally Murphy*

# Setting the Table

May I set the table,
May I pick things up?
May I carry spoons and forks,
And my flower cup?

May I put the jams out,
And the butter, too?
May I set the breakfast table?
May I sit by you?

*—Jane Yolen*

# No Peas

Oh please, no peas, no peas today.
I must try just a few, you say?
No, Aunt, you can't make me eat peas.
An egg I'll beg; let me choose cheese.
I'd eat peas sweet and crunchy raw.
Not these hot peas and that's for sure.
I'd spew and you would hate the smell.
I guess the mess would irk as well.
I can't—I shan't—eat peas. No way.
I won't. I don't care what you say.
My lips are zipped—they're shut quite tight.
No peas will pass through them tonight.

I sniff a whiff of apple pie...
a treat so sweet it makes me sigh.
I find my mind I've changed on peas.
Last one! All gone! Dessert? Yes, please!

*—Teena Raffa-Mulligan*

# Canoe

Skimming through
liquid silver,
watch the surface
shimmer, shiver.
Stir the lake with a giant spoon
and glide across
the rippling moon.

*—Juanita Havill*

# How to Live Forever

No one can live forever. That
Is what the grown-ups told me,
Although they said the end won't come
Till I'm a very old me.

I really do not like this plan,
And I intend to change it
So I can live forever. Here
Is how I will arrange it:

I'll eat a ton of Brussels sprouts
And tons of cauliflower,
To make each second of my life
Feel like it lasts an hour.

And every hour of my life
Will last eternities when
Instead of ice cream, candy, cake,
Or pie, I'll ask for peas. Then

I'll give up dips and chips and fries
And all things fat and creamy.
Eternities will come and go.
I'll stay. And you will see me

Always drinking carrot juice, and
Eating chocolate...never.
No chocolate? NO CHOCOLATE?
Who wants to live forever?

—*Judith Viorst*

# While I Am Asleep in My Bed

I am under my covers, the sun has gone down
My busy day is done
As I close my eyes
Some other folks—instead
Keep busy all night
While I am asleep in my bed

Bakers bake doughnuts, muffins and cakes
Air traffic controllers keep airplanes safe
Taxi drivers move people around
And truck drivers crisscross the town
While I am asleep in my bed

Doctors take care of emergencies
The post office prepares its deliveries
For the alarm's sound a fireman listens
And cleaning crews make offices glisten
While I am asleep in my bed

Hotel clerks check in some sleepyheads
Newspapers are printed so they can be read
Factory workers work straight through the night
Police officers make sure everything's right
While I am asleep in my bed

The sun comes up and I jump to the floor
Morning's at the door
And I am happy to say
I look forward to what's ahead
Thanks to the people who worked all night
While I was asleep in my bed

*—Michael Salinger*

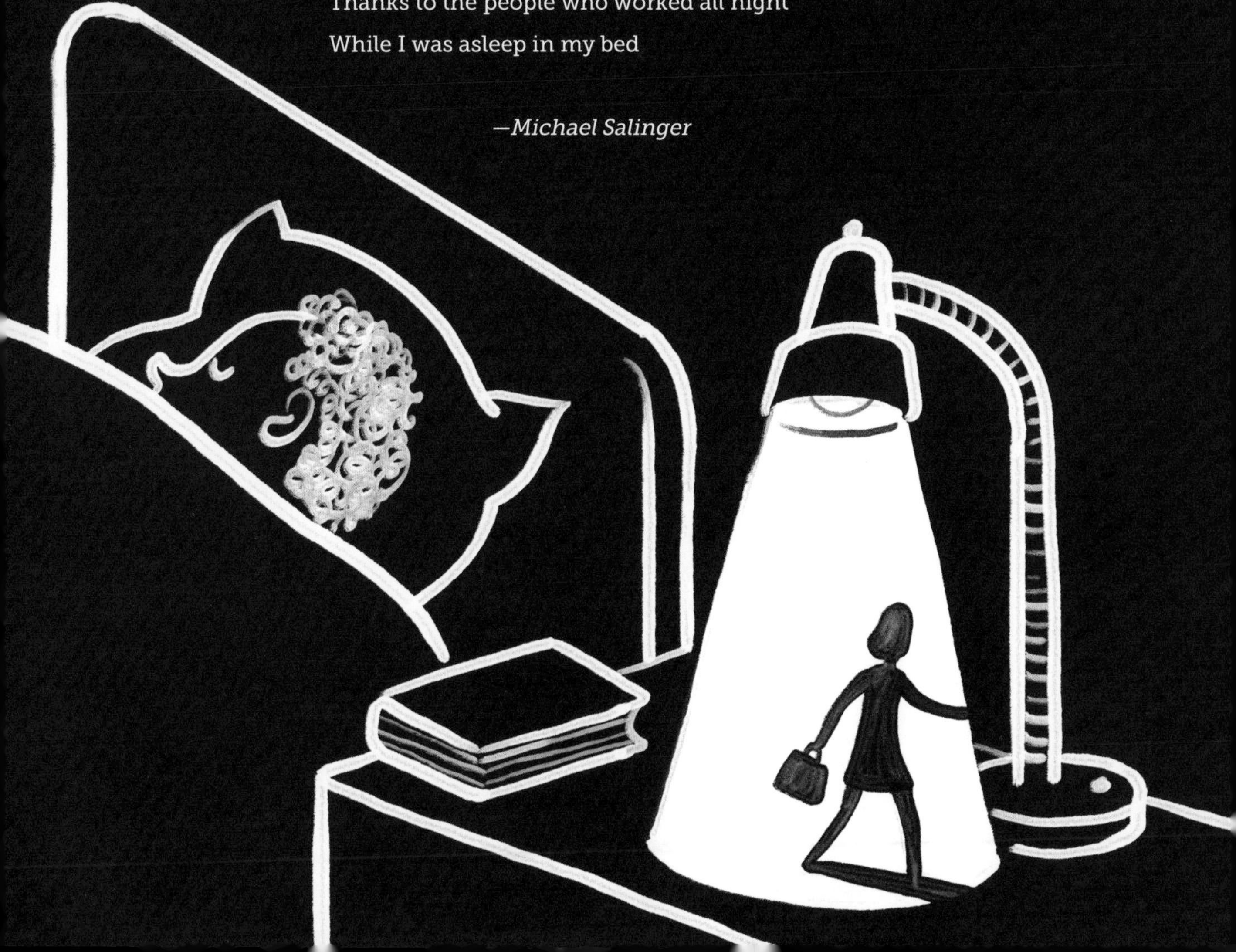

# Air Ships

Like silver sails on silver ships,
A fleet of clouds floats by then slips
Into its Milky Way lagoon
Beneath the lighthouse of the moon.

*—Charles Ghigna*

# Morning Star

If I were a star
of the twinkling kind
surrounded by
diamonds at night

I might be inclined
to wait until dawn
then twinkle
with all of my might

—*Jackie Hosking*

# Night Flight

Close your eyes
so we can fly
around the clouds,
across the sky.

Close your eyes
and hold on tight.
We'll zoom around
the moon tonight.

Close your eyes
and swoop with me
above the dark
and swirly sea.

Close your eyes
so dreams can soar
from pointy peak
to slippery shore.

And when we've been
from star to star,
from here to there,
from near to far,
from top to bottom,
coast to coast,
we'll float back home
for eggs and toast.

*—Ted Scheu*

# Moon Mice

Moon mice are hungry but easy to please.

They know the moon

Is made of cheese,

Deliciously light and delightfully round.

The moon is full.

The mice are bound

To nip and to nibble, to nibble and nosh.

A jolly good dinner,

By golly, by gosh!

They nibble and nip in the middle of night,

Bit by bit,

Bite by bite,

Happily munching, till after a while,

All that is left

Of the moon is a smile.

*—Neal Levin*

# Meeting a Cow

Today I met a cow
coming through the field.

She called to me:
*Moooooooo*

And I called back:
*Moooooooo*

And she replied:
*Moooooooo*

And I agreed:
*Moooooooo*

And presently
and pleasantly

we each went
on
our
way.

—*Sharon Creech*

# Old Ned

I love old Ned
Our barnyard horse,
Swaybacked and blind,
And kind, of course.
He pulled Pa's wagon,
Long ago,
Through springtime rains,
And freezing snow.
Ned pulled the plow,
To till our land,
Now, he eats carrots,
From my hand.
Dad says Ned has earned his keep,
And a nice warm barn,
For his place to sleep.

*—David Davis*

# Armadillo

The armadillo dwells inside
The scaly armor of his hide
And while deep down he's soft and sweet,
He's harder than a city street.
So please don't pick an armadillo
To go to sleep on. Use your pillow.

*—X. J. Kennedy*

# For Pete's Snake

Said Pete, "I made a big mistake
in purchasing a twelve-foot snake.
For shocked was I to get the news
he needed six new pairs of shoes."

*—Linda Knaus*

# My Friend the Chameleon

Have you seen my friend, the chameleon?

Wherever he goes, he blends right in.

Of all the kinds of lizards

He's really quite a wizard

Changing colors magically

To fit in with the scenery.

—*Nina Laden*

# Sandra's Pet

I never know what I should say
if Sandra comes around to play,
for she might bring her pets round, too;
her hamster, mouse and kangaroo.

The hamster always makes me sneeze,
the mouse eats all my bread and cheese.
But, oh, the kangaroo is sweet,
he gives me rides each time we meet.

A kangaroo can bounce, of course,
much higher than the average horse,
and when you ride one hold on tight
and look out for the ceiling light.

Next birthday, if I'm asked which pet
I really, really long to get,
I wouldn't have a second thought
on which would be the nicest sort.

I wouldn't choose a hamster or
a mouse, of that you can be sure.
Instead, I'd go round all the shops
until I found a pet that hops.

So, Sandra, yes, please come to tea,
any time is good for me,
and don't forget to bring with you
your jumpy bumpy kangaroo.

*—Martin Pierce*

# Rock Pool

Stickleback's on bass guitar,
Hermit Crab's on drums,
Starfish does the singing
and a Shrimp guitarist strums.

The hardest-rockin' group around,
come catch us playing live—
but get your ticket quick because
we tour with every tide!



—*Matt Goodfellow*

# I Dreamed I Met a Unicorn

I dreamed I met a unicorn,
whose coat was white as snow.
She had a small and dainty horn.
Her voice was soft, and low.

She spoke of rich and distant lands,
beyond the woodsy track.
She bowed her head. I raised my hands,
and climbed upon her back.

Wind rippled through her silver mane.
She galloped through the sky.
Above the woods, and golden plain,
and fleecy clouds, on high.

When I woke up, that happy dream
still danced inside my head.
Her sparkling hooves! Her eyes that gleam!
Once more, it's time for bed.

Once more, I'll sleep till early morn.
I close my weary eyes,
and hope to ride my unicorn
across the starry skies.

*—Dave Crawley*

# Last Poem

Cuddle cozy.

Listen, look.

Quiet voices.

Bedtime book.

Turning pages,

One by one.

Sleepy kisses

When we're done.

*—Stephanie Calmenson*

# Acknowledgments

**Kenn Nesbitt**: "Whew!," "Poems Can Be Silly," "Have I Told You?," "What Do You Dream?," "Ted, Ted, Climb in Bed," "Say Good Night" and "How to Fall Asleep" copyright © 2016 by Kenn Nesbitt. Used by permission of the author.
**Lisa Wheeler**: "Paper People" copyright © 2016 by Lisa Wheeler. Used by permission of the author.
**Kim Norman**: "I Like Old Stories" copyright © 2016 by Kim Norman. Used by permission of the author.
**Renée LaTulippe**: "If I Were a Blue Balloon" copyright © 2016 Renée M. LaTulippe. All rights reserved.Used by permission of the author.
**Donna Jo Napoli**: "Roar" copyright © 2016 by Donna Jo Napoli. Used by permission of the author.
**Eileen Spinelli**: "Stuffed Animal Collection" copyright © 2016 by Eileen Spinelli. Used by permission of the author.
**Charles Waters**: "Five Little Birds" copyright © 2016 by Charles Waters. Used by permission of the author who controls all rights.
**Jacqueline Jules**: "Pigeon" copyright © 2016 by Jacqueline Jules. Used by permission of the author.
**Betsy Franco**: "Me at the Sea" copyright © 2016 by Betsy Franco. Used by permission of the author, who holds all rights.
**Avis Harley**: "Ocean Fun" copyright © 2016 by Avis Harley. Used by permission of the author.
**Carol-Ann Hoyte**: "Water Can Be a..." copyright © 2016 by Carol-Ann Hoyte. All rights reserved. Used by permission of the author.
**Edel Wignell**: "Gentle Shower" copyright © 2016 The Australian Society of Authors. Used by permission of the author.
**Nikki Grimes**: "Backyard Circus" copyright © 2016 by Nikki Grimes. Used by permission of Curtis Brown, Ltd.
**Sara Holbrook**: "Trampoline" copyright © 2016 by Sara Holbrook. Used by permission of the author.
**Naomi Shihab Nye**: "Map of Fun" copyright © 2014 by Naomi Shihab Nye. Used by permission of the author.
**Santino Panzica**: "Sleepy" copyright © 2016 by Santino Panzica. Used by permission of the author.
**Michael J. Rosen**: "Wave Good Night" copyright © 2016 by Michael J. Rosen. Used by permission of the author.
**Kurt Cyrus**: "The Road to Morning" copyright © 2016 by Kurt Cyrus. Used by permission of the author.
**Jack Prelutsky**: "My Horse Is Floating in the Air" copyright © 2016 by Jack Prelutsky, who controls all rights. Used by permission of the author.
**Dennis Lee**: "The Big Parade" and "Bigger Than Big" copyright © 2016 by Dennis Lee. Used by permission of the author.
**Jon Scieszka**: "All at Once" copyright © 2016 by Jon Scieszka. Used by permission of the author.
**Scott Seegert**: "Dinnertime" copyright © 2016 by Scott Seegert. Used by permission of the author.
**Alan Katz**: "Friends on the Menu" copyright © 2016 by Alan Katz. Used by permission of the author.
**Diane Z. Shore**: "To Market, to Market" copyright © 2016 by Diane Z. Shore. Used by permission of the author.
**Michele Krueger**: "My Uncle Joe" copyright © 2016 by Michele Krueger. Used by permission of the author.
**Margarita Engle**: "Each Day at the Zoo Is Always New" copyright © 2016 by Margarita Engle. Used by permission of the author.
**David L. Harrison**: "Lamb Said, 'Mew'" and "Gesundheit" copyright © 2016 by David L. Harrison. Used by permission of the author.
**Amy Ludwig VanDerwater**: "Our Kittens" copyright © 2016 by Amy Ludwig VanDerwater. Used by permission of Curtis Brown, Ltd.
**Kate Coombs**: "Running" copyright © 2016 by Kate Coombs. Used by permission of the author.
**Timothy Tocher**: "All in a Day's Work" copyright © 2016 by Timothy Tocher. Used by permission of the author.
**Mark Carthew**: "The Dandelion" copyright © 2016 by Mark Carthew. Used by permission of the author.
**John Foster**: "Wind" copyright © 2016 by John Foster. Used by permission of the author.
**Greg Pincus**: "A Hard Rain" copyright © 2016 by Greg Pincus. Used by permission of the author.
**John Rice**: "Starry" copyright © 2015 by John Rice. Used by permission of the author.
**Lorie Ann Grover**: "Toasty, Warm Jammies" copyright © 2016 by Lorie Ann Grover. Used by permission of Curtis Brown, Ltd.
**Ron Koertge**: "Bedtime on 7th Avenue" copyright © 2016 by Ron Koertge. Used by permission of the author.
**Bruce Lansky**: "Sleepless" copyright © 2015 by Bruce Lansky. Used by permission of the author.
**Christine Heppermann**: "A Friend to the Rescue" copyright © 2016 by Christine Heppermann. Used by permission of the author.
**Colin West**: "An Odd Thing Happened..." copyright © 2016 by Colin West. Used by permission of the author. Reprinted with permission.
**Darren Sardelli**: "Our Grandma Kissed a Pumpkin" copyright © 2016 by Darren Sardelli. Used by permission of the author.
**Verla Kay**: "I Have a Hat" copyright © 2016 by Verla Kay. Used by permission of the author.
**B. J. Lee**: "Skateboard Girl" copyright © 2016 by B. J. Lee. Used by permission of the author.
**Libby Martinez**: "The Tadpole Bowl" copyright © 2016 by Libby Martinez. Used by permission of Curtis Brown, Ltd.

**Glenys Eskdale**: "Puppy Morning" copyright © 2016 by Glenys Eskdale. Used by permission of the author.
**Kathryn Apel**: "School Bus" and "My Dad" copyright © 2016 by Kathryn Apel. Used by permission of the author.
**Sydra Mallery**: "First Day, Kindergarten" copyright © 2014 by Sydra Mallery. Used by permission of the author.
**Jen Bryant**: "Hummer" copyright © 2016 by Jen Bryant. Used by permission of the author.
**Sophie Masson**: "Seagull Beach Party" copyright © 2016 by Sophie Masson. Used by permission of the author.
**Meredith Costain**: "An Orchestra in My Room" copyright © 2016 by Meredith Costain. Used by permission of the author.
**Brian P. Cleary**: "God Bless Me" copyright © 2016 by Brian P. Cleary. Used by permission of the author.
**Sherryl Clark**: "River Song" copyright © 2016 by Sherryl Clark. Used by permission of the author.
**Liz Brownlee**: "This Is the Hour" copyright © 2014 by Liz Brownlee. Used by permission of the author.
**Lee Bennett Hopkins**: "Sleepy" copyright © 2016 by Lee Bennett Hopkins. Used by permission of the author.
**Lee Wardlaw**: "It's Routine" copyright © 2016 by Lee Wardlaw. Used by permission of the author.
**Andrea Perry**: "The Seventeen Fitz Sisters" copyright © 2016 by Andrea Perry. Used by permission of the author.
**Samuel Kent**: "Three Bears Aboard an Iceberg" copyright © 2016 by Samuel Kent. Used by permission of the author.
**Linda Ashman**: "On Adopting a Pet Elephant" copyright © 2016 by Linda Ashman. Used by permission of the author.
**Paul Orshoski**: "Grandpa's Hair" copyright © 2016 by Paul Orshoski. Used by permission of the author.
**Celeste Walters**: "Sleeping Over" copyright © 2016 by Celeste Walters. Used by permission of the author.
**April Halprin Wayland**: "Rolling down the Hill" copyright © 2016 by April Halprin Wayland. Used by permission of the author, who controls all rights.
**Celia Warren**: "Socks on the Washing Line" copyright © 2016 by Celia Warren. Used by permission of the author.
**Donna Marie Merritt**: "Me and My Feet" copyright © 2016 by Donna Marie Merritt. Used by permission of the author.
**Heidi Bee Roemer**: "Flower Power!" copyright © 2016 by Heidi Bee Roemer. Used by permission of the author. All rights reserved.
**Bob Raczka**: "Wild Flowers" copyright © 2016 by Bob Raczka. Used by permission of the author.
**Carole Gerber**: "Time to Sleep" and "Snow Angels" copyright © 2015 by Carole Gerber. Used by permission of the author.
**Steven Withrow**: "Counting Rhyme" copyright © 2016 by Steven Withrow. Used by permission of the author. All rights reserved.
**Jenny Erlanger**: "Monkey Business" copyright © 2016 by Jenny Erlanger. Used by permission of the author.
**Matt Forrest Esenwine**: "A Visit to the Forest" copyright © 2016 by Matt Forrest Esenwine. Used by permission of the author.
**Ann Whitford Paul**: "Hippo" copyright © 2016 by Ann Whitford Paul. Used by permission of the author.
**Brenda Williams**: "Baby's Bath Time" copyright © 2016 by Brenda Williams. Used by permission of the author.
**Sonya Sones**: "Boof" copyright © 2016 by Sonya Sones. Used by permission of the author.
**Eric Ode**: "Bath Time" copyright © 2016 by Eric Ode. Used by permission of the author.
**Calef Brown**: "The Suit" copyright © 2015 by Calef Brown. Used by permission of the author.
**Tiffany Strelitz Haber**: "PB Patty" copyright © 2016 by Tiffany Strelitz Haber. Used by permission of the author.
**Ralph Fletcher**: "Good-Night Poem" copyright © 2016 by Ralph Fletcher. Used by permission of the author.
**Robert Pottle**: "Wiggle Wiggle" copyright © 2016 by Robert Pottle. Used by permission of the author.
**Robert Schechter**: "The 'Just Because' Hug" copyright © 2016 by Robert Schechter. Used by permission of the author.
**J. Patrick Lewis**: "The Song of the Littlest Cat" copyright © 2012 by J. Patrick Lewis. Used by permission of the author.
**Rebecca Kai Dotlich**: "Sky Story" copyright © 2016 by Rebecca Kai Dotlich. Used by permission of Curtis Brown, Ltd.
**Pat Mora**: "Happy Visits" copyright © 2016 by Pat Mora. Used by permission of Curtis Brown, Ltd.
**Laura Purdie Salas**: "We're Bats" copyright © 2016 by Laura Purdie Salas. Used by permission of the author, who controls all rights.
**Elaine Magliaro**: "Crickets" copyright © 2016 by Elaine Magliaro. Used by permission of the author.
**Betsy R. Rosenthal**: "Rainbow" copyright © 2016 by Betsy R. Rosenthal. Used by permission of the author, who controls all rights.
**Dianne Bates**: "Tasty Moon" copyright © 2016 by Dianne Bates. Used by permission of the author.
**Nancy Willard**: "The Banquet of the Sun" copyright © 2014 by Nancy Willard. Used by permission of the author.
**Joan Bransfield Graham**: "Tuck a Poem in Your Head" copyright © 2016 by Joan Bransfield Graham. Used by permission of the author, who controls all rights.